SHERRI L. KING

Caress
OF
FLAME

ELLORA'S CAVE
ROMANTICA PUBLISHING

An Ellora's Cave Romantica Publication

www.ellorascave.com

Caress of Flame

ISBN 9781419956317
ALL RIGHTS RESERVED.
Caress of Flame Copyright © 2006 Sherri L. King
Edited by Kelli Kwiatkowski
Cover art by Darrell King

Electronic book Publication August 2006
Trade paperback Publication May 2007

Excerpt from *Ride the Lightning* Copyright © 2006 Sherri L. King

Content Advisory:

S – ENSUOUS
E – ROTIC
X – TREME

Ellora's Cave Publishing offers three levels of Romantica® reading entertainment: S (S-ensuous), E (E-rotic), and X (X-treme).

The following material contains graphic sexual content meant for mature readers. This story has been rated E–rotic.

S-*ensuous* love scenes are explicit and leave nothing to the imagination.

E-*rotic* love scenes are explicit, leave nothing to the imagination, and are high in volume per the overall word count. E-rated titles might contain material that some readers find objectionable—in other words, almost anything goes, sexually. E-rated titles are the most graphic titles we carry in terms of both sexual language and descriptiveness in these works of literature.

X-*treme* titles differ from E-rated titles only in plot premise and storyline execution. Stories designated with the letter X tend to contain difficult or controversial subject matter not for the faint of heart.

Also by Sherri L. King

80

Bachelorette

Beyond Illusion

Ellora's Cavemen: Tales from the Temple III (*anthology*)

Ferocious

Fetish

Manaconda (*anthology*)

Midnight Desires (*anthology*)

Moon Lust 1: Moonlust

Moon Lust 2: Bitten

Moon Lust 3: Mating Season

Moon Lust 4: Feral Heat

Rayven's Awakening

Sanctuary

Shikar 2: Ride the Lightning

Sin and Salvation

Sterling Files 1: Steele

Sterling Files 2: Vicious

Sterling Files 3: Fyre

Sterling Files 4: Hyde

The Horde Wars 1: Ravenous

The Horde Wars 2: Wanton Fire

The Horde Wars 3: Razors Edge

The Horde Wars 4: Lord of the Deep

The Jewel

Full Moon Xmas

About the Author

ဢ

Sherri L. King lives in the American Deep South with her husband, artist and illustrator Darrell King. Critically acclaimed author of The Horde Wars and Moon Lust series, her primary interests lie in the world of action packed paranormals, though she's been known to dabble in several other genres as time permits.

Sherri welcomes comments from readers. You can find her website and email address on her author bio page at www.ellorascave.com.

Tell Us What You Think

We appreciate hearing reader opinions about our books. You can email us at Comments@EllorasCave.com.

CARESS OF FLAME

ဆ

Dedication

∞

For D

Trademarks Acknowledgement

∞

The author acknowledges the trademarked status and trademark owners of the following wordmarks mentioned in this work of fiction:

Jagermeister: Mast-Jagermeister Aktiengesellschaft Corporation

Victoria's Secret: Victoria's Secret Partnership

Yoo-hoo: Yoo-hoo Beverage Company Corporation

Chapter One

✆

Isis sat before the enormous lighted mirror and sipped from her hot, creamy latté. It was as sweet as a candy bar—she'd put a ton of sugar in it—and it was just the way she liked her coffee. Isis knew that soon she'd be buzzing with energy, which was very good since she was due to go out onto the stage in an hour and she'd need every ounce of energy she could muster to put on a good show.

In her other hand Isis held a crumpled envelope, clutching it tight. She needed to be doing her hair and makeup for the show, but she couldn't let go of the letter. Her sister's letter. The sister she hadn't heard from since she'd set out on the road at seventeen nearly ten years ago. How Maria had found her was a miracle in itself. She had no idea how her sister had done it. Isis had always been so careful, keeping her phone number unlisted, changing it every six months or so. Her address was listed as a P.O. box and she moved around a lot, leaving no clues to her true addresses.

At least, for now, she had the peace of mind to know that Maria and especially her stepfather had no idea where she actually lived. But just in case, she had already decided to move.

Just in case.

Isis set her cup of coffee down and ran her hand through her long red hair. It was tangled and clumped in large, unruly locks—the day had been humid and rainy—and she winced as her fingers passed through the knots. She wished her hair would decide what it wanted to do. Some days it was so straight it was like a silk waterfall down her back and others it was a frizzy mess that could only be tamed with hours of work. Isis crumpled the paper tight in her fist once more before putting it in the front pocket of her jeans and grabbing the nearest hairbrush to begin her preparation for work.

A hundred strokes later—and with a little help from a professional-grade ceramic hair straightener—and her hair was smooth as satin, shining like liquid, falling almost to her waist. Her hair, she knew, was what drew so many of her faithful customers and she was fine with that. Whatever they liked, she liked, because it meant more money for her and less worry about finances.

Not that Isis had had much worry over finances in the past year since she'd begun working at The Pink Pit. She made lots of money each night that she performed— so much it still sometimes surprised her. But it was hard to let go of old habits and she'd worried about money for so many years it seemed almost ingrained in her to keep doing it. She hated that about herself. Among other things.

It was time for her makeup—this part she truly hated the most. She'd never been clever enough to use cosmetics to enhance her features. Most of her life she'd gone natural, without any makeup at all. Picking up her thick kohl pencil, she leaned closer to the mirror and put a dark ring around the edges of her hazel eyes, trying her best to keep a steady hand. This made her eyes look impossibly large—innocent even. Isis knew it was part of her allure...even if it was fake. She finished the effect with a generous application of black mascara that enhanced her already super-long eyelashes.

She put on her favorite lipstick, a burgundy hue so as not to clash with her vivid hair color, and studied her face thoroughly. It looked acceptable enough despite her large nose and overly full lips. Anyway, the customers wouldn't be looking much at her less-than-beautiful face. And with that thought she went to the large wardrobe at the end of the ample communal powder room. She delved inside it, looking at the various garish and revealing garments until she found exactly what she'd been looking for.

A pair of black PVC Daisy Duke shorts, a purple PVC bra and a short black leather jacket to complete the ensemble. As Isis dressed in her chosen costume for the night ahead, she carefully folded her own jeans so that her sister's note didn't fall out and go missing. Isis wanted to hold onto it for a little bit longer yet.

"Girl, you look downright dangerous tonight," Rebecca, one of the other girls that worked at The Pink Pit, said as she sashayed into the room.

Isis forced a smile. She wasn't exactly a people person—except when up on the stage performing. Rebecca was nice, she knew, but it was still hard to even engage in small talk with someone else, Isis had become so used to being a loner. "Thanks Becca, it's the look I was going for," she managed.

"Well congratulations, you look like you could take on every man out there." Rebecca sat before the mirror and began applying her long, dark, fake eyelashes.

Isis ran the brush through her hair one last time. It was now only five minutes before she was due onstage.

This was the worst part of the job—the anticipation. What would happen up there? There was the possibility of many things, not all of them pleasant, and Isis wished that she could see into the future, just this once, to be sure of her success—or failure—for the night.

"Don't look so serious, Isis," Rebecca told her gently. "I know you're shy around people—hell, all of us have noticed that about you—but you don't have a thing to worry about tonight. You're the shining star of that stage out there. People come here just to see you. You're so talented I can't imagine why you would worry before a performance, but I see you do it before each and every show. Now stop it." She finished with a smile.

Isis smiled again and said nothing. She took a deep, calming breath and made her way out of the powder room and into the backstage area, where two big, muscular guys in skintight black T-shirts and jeans that left nothing to the imagination were waiting. Isis nodded to them, acknowledging their presence, safe in the knowledge that the two brutish men would do anything to keep her safe. It was their job after all.

"Friends, let me proudly introduce the highlight of tonight, the Great Goddess Isis."

Isis heard the announcement on the loudspeaker just beyond the curtain and took one last long, soothing breath, steeling herself for what would come next.

"Haunted", by Evanescence—her choice of music for the night's performance—began to play and Isis sashayed out onto the stage with a sexy confidence she did not feel. The lights were bright, obscuring her sight of the audience beyond the stage. She could hear the cheers and jeers plainly, even over the incredibly loud music she had chosen. Playing the part she had almost perfected, she slinked up to the pole that stood in the middle of the stage and began to dance around it.

Isis imagined that she was a pagan from ancient times, dancing for the pleasure of the gods who would ensure good fortune, abundant crops and long life. Perhaps this dance was for the benefit of the true Goddess Isis herself. This kept her mind off what she was really doing as Isis shed her leather jacket and climbed up the pole. Isis swung around, holding the pole between her legs as she fell backward, her long hair reaching to the floor. A loud cheer went up, interrupting her concentration, but she quickly blocked out the sound and instead let the melody of the music entrance her as she continued her dance.

Isis slid down the pole, slowly, sensually. She landed on her feet and walked down the length of the stage where dozens of hands were holding out green bills. She undulated, she twirled, she kicked and shook her hair wildly about her and the crowd's cheers rose to a roar that echoed in her ears. With a thrust of her hips and a practiced move of her arm, she removed her tight shorts, revealing a black thong that only barely concealed her shaven pussy. She bent close to the men and let them put money in her panties then rose and resumed dancing.

The music rose to a crescendo and Isis shrugged out of her bra, revealing her large, round, rose-crested natural breasts. They shook and bounced as she danced and the crowd, if possible, went even wilder. She took to the pole again, slinking around it, rubbing her body against it like she would a lover. More hands waved at the perimeter of the stage, shaking money back and forth, and after a few seconds more with the pole she danced closer and closer to the edge of the stage, letting dozens of hands shove green slips of paper in her panties.

The music ended and the lights went down on the stage. She grabbed fistfuls of money that were still being waved at her. When her hands were full she gave the crowd a large smile and retreated behind the stage curtain once more. One of the bouncers went onto the stage after her and collected her discarded clothing. Not that it mattered. Isis made it a point never to wear the same thing twice.

It felt like a long walk back to the powder room. This was only the first of three appearances she would make tonight, but already she felt wiped out. Exhausted. There were three other girls in the room when Isis returned, but she barely paid them any heed. She sat before the mirror, naked but for her black thong, and counted out the money she had collected from the eager men she'd entertained. More than three hundred dollars already. If the trend continued she calculated that she could very well make a thousand dollars tonight. She'd made more before, but this was, after all, a weekday. She was happy with what she'd earned thus far.

It would be another half hour before she was due back onstage. Isis sat back in her chair and stared off into space, imagining she was somewhere else, someone else living somewhere magical where she would have no worries or cares. Isis would sit this way until the last ten minutes before the show, when she would select her next outfit from the wardrobe. No one spoke to her and she kept her own silence, ignoring the conversations taking place around her. It was lonely, probably rude, and she knew the other girls thought she was strange, but she didn't care.

Loneliness was a welcome companion, as it had been for many years. The pain of it had long since become something of a comfort. Isis knew she was alone—completely alone—and that was just as she liked it.

Chapter Two

ɞ

Isis stopped for gas and went inside the station to buy a Yoo-hoo. She always celebrated a successful night with a Yoo-hoo. She absolutely loved them. It was three-thirty in the morning and there was no one about. It was quiet but for the chirping of the crickets—their last call to mate before cold weather interrupted them. The station was a large one, with bright lights and several pumps. It was situated in a very lightly populated area and there were woods surrounding the store on three sides, giving it an eerie look and feel at such a dark hour.

She made her purchase and paid for her gas, only murmuring when the clerk told her to have a nice night. Isis bent her head so that a fall of hair obscured her face as she walked away. When she exited the station she first heard the crickets, and the wind, which had picked up a little. Beyond that, so faint Isis thought for a moment that she imagined it, came the sounds of a scuffle in the dark patch of trees beyond the reach of the gas station's overly bright lights.

The last thing she wanted to do was get involved in some kind of gang fight. Were there even gangs here in this unpopulated area? She couldn't be sure, but whatever they were, the sounds of the battle grew louder as if their fight was bringing them closer to the gas station.

Against her better judgment, Isis walked in the direction of the fight. She didn't know why she did it, only that she felt compelled to see what all the fuss was about. She approached the border of the trees and stared hard into the darkness.

A bright explosion of fire lit the night sky. It was so big and so powerful that Isis felt the heat of it on her face and felt its wind ruffle her hair. It blinded her for a moment, but when her vision cleared of its dancing spots she made out the form of a man bending over the lifeless lump of his fallen adversary. She couldn't see the man's face, it was far too dark for that, but she clearly saw the outline of his body. It was almost as if he had a faint glow about him...or coming from within him.

Isis shook her head to clear it of such fanciful thoughts and watched the man move even closer to the fallen one. With one violent thrust the man plunged his fist into the chest of the unconscious man. It must had taken a superhuman effort to do this, Isis knew, but still she saw him pull the heart from the cavity he'd beaten into his enemy. With a loud, squishy sound the heart was in his hand, all black and gooey, and then it burst into flame.

She must have made some sound, some movement that alerted him to her presence. The man looked up and Isis froze. She still couldn't see his face clearly, but his eyes glowed golden orange in the darkness and he had to stand almost seven feet tall. Isis dropped her Yoo-hoo in surprise and the glass shattered on the rough pavement. The sound seemed to spur the man on and he began to approach her.

Isis immediately turned and sprinted full out to her car. She locked the doors as soon as she got in and cranked the engine with trembling fingers. Isis backed up at a wild speed, not even looking behind her for obstacles. She saw the man pause at the border of trees and she saw that his hair was long—way too long for a man—and dark as pitch. She slammed on the brakes and put her car in drive, turning around in the parking lot at a speed that stunned even her. She pulled out onto the road and stomped her gas pedal to the floor, speeding away as if the hounds of hell were yapping at her heels.

It took several minutes of very fast driving before Isis had calmed herself down enough to go over what she'd just seen. Had the dark man *really* pulled the heart out of the chest of the other? How was such a thing even possible? She'd never in her life seen such a casual display of power. The dark man hadn't even struggled to remove his enemy's heart. He'd punched right through the rib cage. It was incredible, but Isis knew what she'd seen hadn't been pretend. Their battle had been very real, with a very grisly end, and she'd been unfortunate enough to witness it.

The first thing that popped into her mind was that she should call the police. Then her dislike of social interaction made her change her mind. She didn't want to deal with the police, not tonight, not ever really. Besides, who would even believe her when Isis told them what she'd seen? Isis knew whoever she told her story to would think she'd gone mental or something. If it was a man she told, he'd no doubt think she just had bad PMS. If it was a woman…Isis didn't know. Should she tell or not?

Not. She didn't want to be involved any more than she already was. If the dark man could pull the heart from a body then she wanted nothing else to do with him, even if it meant bringing him to justice.

And then there was the fact that she had *seen* the heart go up in flames in the dark man's hand. Isis had no explanation for that. Only question after question. How had he done it? She hadn't seen him strike a match or flick a lighter. And how had he held the flames within his palm without being burned? Isis had no rational explanation for these questions and she knew for a fact that no one would believe that part of the story if she told it. Hell, *she* hardly believed that she'd seen it.

Perhaps it had been a trick. What kind of trick she couldn't guess, but there was just no way a man could do what the dark man had done so effortlessly. No way.

Isis slowed her car, not wanting to get a ticket for her clumsy attempt at a getaway. She was tired of trying to rationalize what she'd seen. It was over now. Isis was growing calmer. There was no need for her to ever think of it again. Besides, she had another crisis on her hands to worry about.

With that reminder, the letter her sister had sent seemed to burn her from its safe place deep in her pocket. She'd read it over a dozen times already and the words had seared themselves into her brain. Why Maria had gone through such obvious trouble to reach her, Isis couldn't guess. Maria had always had a mean streak in her. Isis knew this well from childhood, when it had been Maria who was the favored child in the family. Two years younger than Isis, Maria hadn't been the angel her mother and stepfather had believed her to be. Isis had been blamed for many of Maria's misdeeds all through grade school — her parents had never even contemplated that Maria might have been at fault, not even once. Isis had paid, and dearly, for what her sister had done in malice. And this tattered piece of paper, this horrible missive, was just another malicious act in Isis' eyes.

It was so hard for her to believe the words of the letter. After all the suffering she had gone through while living with her family, Isis couldn't believe the latest turn of events.

Only two years had passed since her mother had died of leukemia. Isis had found out about her mother's death through a distant relative she'd met by chance one day in a department store. The news had hit Isis hard and she'd suffered through a bad depression because of it, but this news from her sister made that time of sadness seem like a trip to an amusement park in comparison.

It was a thirty-minute drive by highway to the small house Isis rented deep in the woods. There were no neighbors anywhere close—that was why Isis had chosen to rent it in the first place. But now, as she finally made it home and pulled into her long gravel driveway, it seemed really creepy. She put her car in park and sat for several long moments, staring into the trees that were illuminated by her headlights, before she sighed heavily and finally turned the ignition off, casting the woods back into their natural darkness.

Trying not to admit her fear by running up to the front door like a great big chicken, she slowly took one step after another until she was on her front porch, unlocking her door with purposefully steady fingers. The wind was cool and she realized as the air hit her face that she had been sweating. Wiping a hand over her face rebelliously, she went into the house and shut the door firmly behind her.

First thing, Isis shed her clothes and climbed into the shower, just as she did every night after a show. She wanted to wash away the feel of all those grabbing hands from her skin. Scrubbing her skin raw was the only way she could feel clean on a night like this. And there was an even greater dirty feeling tonight due to Maria's letter.

Isis thought she'd become numb over the years. But the note had brought out all the old feelings of fear and rage as if no time had passed at all. She felt like she was a teenager again, hiding from her stepfather and dealing with her mother's bipolar condition every second of every day. It sickened her, this weakness she hadn't been able to conquer, even after all this time.

How she'd hated her stepfather. How she had loved her mother, wanting nothing but to please her and always failing. She still hated her stepdad—more now after reading Maria's note—and she still loved her mother, forgiving her for all the hardships Isis had endured because her mother had been mentally unstable. Maria had never been the object of their mother's rage, only Isis. Even as a child Isis liked to stand on the fringe of things, to blend into obscurity as often as she could, especially when her stepfather was around. Their mother had always seen this as a failure in Isis and it still hurt to think about, even now, so long after the horror of life with her family.

What hurt Isis the most was the fact that her mother had gone to the grave without believing the truth. No, her mother had chosen her husband over her child, and Isis knew nothing could have persuaded her mother to believe the truth. Isis had had to leave after that horrible winter night just two days after her seventeenth birthday. Life in her stepfather's home would have been impossible after the traumatic events of that long-ago night anyway.

The pain of her childhood had shaped her into the loner she was now, and Isis knew it. She hated to hear people blame their parents for their problems, but Isis secretly *did* blame her parents. Or her stepfather, at least. Isis often used to wonder what she would be like today if she'd only had better parents, but she'd long ago given up that path of thought. It did no good to ask, "What if?" What if had no bearing on the present and Isis had eventually accepted that.

Or so she'd thought.

Damn her sister. And damn her stepfather. Isis had left them both behind and never looked back. Why had Maria felt it necessary to tell Isis the horrible news?

Again, though it pained her, Isis admitted to herself that it had been out of malice. What else could she believe? The contents of the letter were only grisly descriptions of things best not thought about—best not even imagined in nightmares. Isis could have died happily not knowing the news the missive contained.

After her shower, Isis retrieved the letter and grabbed a half-full bottle of Jagermeister from the fridge. She opened the bottle and drank from it, not bothering to get a glass. The liquor burned its way down her throat, filling her mouth with the taste of licorice and warming her throughout. Isis took two more large swallows and sat at her kitchen table, laying out the paper before her.

Isis stared off into space, imagining herself somewhere else, *anywhere* else. Every few minutes she'd take a drag from the bottle of Jager, until her head was abuzz with the warmth of a good bout of drunkenness.

She eventually passed out, her head falling to the table, her face pressed on the rumpled letter. The now-empty bottle of Jagermeister fell unheeded to the floor beside her chair and then all fell silent within the house.

* * * * *

Isis woke up in her bed just as the sun was going down. She'd had strange dreams all night, of men fighting and burning hearts and her sister fat and pregnant with a self-satisfied grin on her face. Isis frowned as memories from the previous night became clearer in her mind.

How had she gotten into her bed?

"What the fuck?" she asked aloud to no one. Thankfully she heard no reply, imagined or real.

Isis was still in her bathrobe and her head ached from too much liquor, but she was certain to a point that she'd been at her kitchen table when she'd passed out. Had she been sleepwalking? Is that how she now found herself in bed? Isis had never done it before so she didn't know how to tell if she had been.

Whatever. At least she'd slept the entire afternoon. That in itself was a blessing—she hardly ever slept a whole day. In fact, she usually lived on a few hours of sleep, no more. Sometimes a sound outside would wake her and she'd be up the rest of the day, checking the locks on her windows and doors, keeping her drapes closed so that the interior of the house was cast in a constant shadow. Other times she just couldn't make herself sleep, no matter how tired she might be. And when she did sleep it was broken by nightmares and a constant sense of dread, waking her up every couple of hours.

Rising with a wince for her aching head, she dressed for the evening, wearing simple jeans and an oversized poet-style shirt. She took two aspirin for her hangover and made her way to the kitchen. Isis was due at work in an hour and she had just enough time to make a grilled cheese sandwich and some tomato soup and scarf it down. Never in her recent memory had she slept so late as this.

It took moments to grab her purse and her keys and leave, locking the door tight behind her. It was an old habit, even though she doubted there was anyone near who would want to plunder her sparsely decorated home. But then again, one never knows, so she always made it a point to lock up as she left.

The hairs on the back of her neck stood up. Isis clutched her purse to her chest and looked around suspiciously. She had the distinct feeling that she was being watched. The woods surrounding her house were dark and impenetrable to the naked eye. Isis couldn't see much of anything, but she still couldn't shake the creeping feeling that somewhere, eyes were following her every movement.

As she approached her car she could have sworn she heard a twig snap in the woods. She hurriedly unlocked the driver's side door and climbed into her car. Laying her head against the steering wheel, she gave a heavy sigh. She was growing too paranoid. It had to be because of her sister's letter, and maybe, just maybe, because of the strange sights she'd seen the night before. Isis lifted her head and slammed her hands against the steering wheel in frustration.

"Quit being such a loser," she told herself firmly as she started the car. "Pretty soon you'll think you're being stalked."

But the feeling of being watched didn't lessen as she pulled out of her driveway. The drive to The Pink Pit seemed to take forever, and when she pulled into her parking space behind the club the hairs on the back of her neck once again rose in alarm.

"What the hell?" She threw open her car door and stepped out. She turned in a circle, looking every which way for some sign that someone was watching her. Of course she saw nothing and berated herself for being so damned paranoid. Still, she walked a little faster than normal to the back entrance of the club.

Once inside she felt safer. There were half a dozen bouncers in the place and it was a very popular club, full of people. If anyone was stalking her, they couldn't hurt her here. Isis pushed the thought of an imaginary stalker far from her mind and focused on the night ahead instead.

Going through the motions of readying herself for the stage like an automaton, Isis didn't even give the other girls in the powder room a passing glance. Tonight, for her first show, she wore a flowing white dress with a virginal, white, lacy bra and a white thong that was nothing but a scrap of cloth. It clearly showed her pussy and that would earn her a lot more money tonight. Or at least she hoped so.

When it was her turn to go out onto the stage, Isis almost froze. That feeling of being watched, of being the subject of a very hungry gaze, had come back with brute force. She was nearly immobilized by fear for a few long seconds and then Isis forced herself to pass the curtain and enter the stage, still breathless with worry.

Of course someone was watching her, Isis chided herself. She was a stripper. Dozens of eyes watched her every night. With this reminder, she threw herself into her routine.

She skipped to the center of the stage to give her virginal look a more authentic feel for her audience. However, she shattered that illusion when she did a slow back flip, revealing her crotch to the crowd, and skillfully unzipped the back of her dress.

Her virginal attire slipped unheeded to the floor. She danced, undulating her hips suggestively, letting her breasts bob with each movement, and casually unhooked the front clasp of her bra. Isis then made a great show of taking off her bra, throwing it into the crowd. Money waved wildly about the stage and Isis bent to let several men stuff bills into her panties. She saw even more waving and knew that tonight she'd make a lot of money.

What she didn't see was the six and a half foot, two hundred and fifty pounds of muscle marching up to the stage. She finally saw him when the dark man shoved some of her customers to the side and approached her, climbing onto the stage.

Isis backed up, knowing the bouncers behind her were coming forward to escort the giant off the stage. But her eyes never left his—they were pale yellow with an orange fire in the center. They burned right through her, as if he could see into her soul. His hair caught her eye then—it was so long and so straight. It shone like a mirror and was so black as to be almost blue in the bright lights of the stage.

Jack, the first bouncer to reach the dark man, put his arm out to stop him from getting any closer to Isis. With one well-practiced move the dark man grabbed Jack's hand and karate chopped his arm. Isis, as well as everyone else around the stage, heard the sound of Jack's arm breaking, even over the loud music still playing. The dark man shoved Jack off the stage and into the crowd.

Shrieks sounded out and the music stopped. The lights came up in the club, blinding everyone for a second except for Isis, who was still framed by the spotlight. She stood frozen, unable to move. As if watching a play she stared, dazed, as the second bouncer, Mike, came forward and made a grab for the dark man. The dark man felled the bouncer with nothing but a punch to his jaw. Mike went down hard and the man advanced.

Isis' paralysis broke and she turned to run. Something hit her with the force of a battering ram. She was spun around by hands stronger than any human's she'd ever come across and thrown roughly, unceremoniously over the dark man's shoulder. In a growing panic Isis beat at his back and buttocks, unavoidably noticing how hard and muscular the giant was.

Another bouncer had reached them. The dark man grabbed the bouncer by the neck and, with an almost casual flick of his wrist, threw him several feet across the room, tables and chairs spilling as the bouncer landed. Hard.

Isis roared and sank her teeth into the lower back of her captor, gagging as the dark man's hair filled her mouth along with his flesh. The man didn't even flinch.

Chaos ruled the club. People everywhere were running for the exits. Another bouncers carefully approached them. Isis could see him out of the corner of her eye. She continued to pummel the dark man, but none of her blows seemed to even faze him as he let the bouncers get closer. She rose up, putting her hands on the dark man's back so that she could look over his shoulder. What she saw froze her heart with fear.

The dark man raised his hand, palm out, and pulled it back as if he were about to pitch a baseball—then an incredibly hot burst of air exploded out of his hand and sent the bouncer flying backward, helpless. Isis felt the heat of that strange wind and she knew immediately that this was the man she'd seen the night before. She remembered that heart exploding into fire in the dark man's palm and at once knew a true, very elemental fear.

Isis bucked wildly, trying to dislodge herself. The man put his hand on her ass—his skin was so *hot*—and effectively stilled her panicked movements. More bouncers approached, but none were foolish enough to get too close to the man who held her captive. Soon all the bouncers who worked in the club surrounded them and Isis felt sure that, with their combined strength, they could free her from this frightening man.

The world fell away and Isis screamed as the sensation of incredible speed overcame her. The G-force pressed her legs against the man's muscular chest. He still hadn't taken his hand from her ass and for some reason that was the most noticeable thing in the strange nothingness Isis found herself flying through. She felt a sick clenching of her stomach and the next thing she knew they were standing in a room she'd never seen before.

Isis was unceremoniously thrown onto the softest, largest bed she'd ever seen. An article of clothing was tossed in her face.

"I'll leave while you dress," the man said in a voice that made her instantly wet. She tamped down on her very unexpected spurt of desire, reminding herself of what this man could do to her if he so chose. Without another word, the dark man turned and left the room, audibly locking the door behind him.

Isis jumped off the bed and flew toward the door he'd passed through. She tried the handle, just to be certain, and sure enough it was locked tight. The door was made of some kind of stone and it looked really heavy, so she knew she couldn't force it open by ramming it with her body or anything like that. But no way was she staying here. There had to be a way out. There was one other door in the room—a closet she guessed, but she would have to investigate to be sure.

"Let me out, you psycho," she screamed through the door, hoping the dark man could hear her beyond it. There was no reply.

"Fuck." She spat out her favorite curse word and kicked the door rebelliously. She was wearing her white stilettos but the kick still hurt her toes and she cursed again.

Her nipples were hard and cold. After being pressed to that man's superhot—*literally* hot—body, she felt bereft and chilled. She grabbed the article of clothing he'd thrown at her. It was a sixties-style baby doll dress.

Isis thought it very weird for a guy to have something like that. Unless he'd done this before, with other girls not unlike her.

Would he kill her? She didn't know. Would he rape her? God, with a voice like that he'd only have to talk to seduce her, but still, the idea scared the shit out of her. She hadn't had sex since...well, that was a train of thought she refused to follow.

Isis put the dress on and began to look for a way to escape, hoping that the man wouldn't return before she found her way out of the room.

Chapter Three

∞

The other stone door in the bedroom didn't open into a closet as she had first suspected. It led, surprisingly, to a very spacious apartment. There were no windows anywhere that she could find and a door that she assumed led out of the apartment but which, of course, was locked tight when she tried the massive...God, was it *gold*?...handle.

The apartment itself was a wonder to her. It was like nothing she'd ever seen before. The ceilings were so high that the light didn't reach the top and it was cast in darkness and eerie shadow. And the lights—they were so strange. The lamps didn't use light bulbs, at least none like any she'd ever seen. Instead, strange orbs of light floated serenely beneath the lampshades, providing all the illumination that the room needed. The walls and floor were made of stone, as was the furniture and bed. All Isis could think was that it must have been a bitch moving all that heavy stone into the dwelling.

There was little artwork in the apartment, but it wasn't needed. All the stone—the doors, the bed, the chairs and tables—were carved with beautiful depictions of what looked like elaborate Celtic knot work and fairy tale creatures. Thick rugs covered the stone floor, pretty things with lovely shades of gold and red and black. It was definitely a masculine dwelling—she could tell that by the color scheme alone.

The air smelled sweet, almost like eucalyptus, and the temperature was perfect. Not too hot, not too cool, just right. There was a dining area but no kitchen that she could find. And there was an incredibly beautiful bathroom all done in stone, with a sunken tub, beautiful sinks, a bidet and a strange-looking toilet.

Isis went through the apartment three times before she gave up and plopped down in one of the great stone chairs. They looked like thrones with plump cushions on them. Isis punched one of the cushions and growled with her frustration, afraid that the man would come back. Afraid that maybe he *wouldn't* come back and she'd die of starvation.

"Don't be stupid," she told herself. "You should be worried he'll come back with a hatchet or something."

But he wouldn't need a hatchet. Isis had seen and felt the strength in him. He could kill her with one blow, she was certain of it.

Would he beat her? Kill her? Why had he kidnapped her? There were a thousand and one questions she kept asking herself and she had no answers to any of them. She would just have to wait to find out what her fate was to be. "The story of my life, man," she said aloud. The sound of her voice, meant to help comfort her, only made her more aware of how alone she really was.

She looked expectantly at the bedroom door, wondering when he might return. One thing was certain—no way did she want that bed anywhere nearby when the dark man returned. She'd just stay here, in what must be the sitting room, and let him come find her.

Isis looked around for a weapon. A candlestick, a vase, *anything*, so long as it was hard and heavy and strong enough to knock her captor out. If she could even get that close to him...Isis wasn't sure if she should wish for that or not. She settled for a strange-looking stick that had been propped against the wall. It was a lovely walking stick, carved elaborately and encrusted with semiprecious stones, and some stones that she would have sworn were real. Like diamond and ruby and tanzanite. She gripped it hard in her hands and took a few practice swings, using it like she might a baseball bat.

The sound of the bedroom door opening alerted her. Isis quickly moved to stand behind the frame of the door that led into the sitting room and waited for him to pass through it.

She saw him come to the doorway and pause. Had he seen her? She didn't think so. But it was obvious that he was being cautious.

"Put that down." His lips tickled her ear.

Isis shrieked. How had he done that? He hadn't come through the door, he'd just appeared at her side. She backed away from him and raised her weapon.

"That scepter was my father's. He was a member of the Council and it was a symbol of his rank. I would be very...displeased if you damaged it," he told her carefully, advancing almost infinitesimally toward her with his hand outstretched.

Isis paused, responding to the gentle caress of his magical voice. Then she gripped the scepter tighter. "Fuck it," she said and swung it with all her might.

The man merely plucked it from her fingers. This enraged Isis, his show of casual power, and she flew at him in a fury. She punched him, kicked him, pulled his hair and bit his nipple through the strange material of his shirt. He gently grabbed her and held her so close she could no longer move, so she spat in his face instead.

"Let me go," she said through a curtain of her tangled hair with a calm she did not feel.

"I am only keeping you from hurting yourself," he said, holding her with one arm as he gently placed his father's scepter against the wall.

His voice was making her nipples hard and her cunt wet. She fought furiously against the reaction but there was no use. Her body's response was far beyond her control.

"What do you want with me?" she asked, hating herself for the tremor she heard in her voice.

His strange eyes seemed to glow from within. His face was so close she could have kissed him. Her spittle glistened on his cheek and for some reason she couldn't fathom, she wanted to gently wipe it away and apologize. One thing was certain. He was a beautiful man. There was no other word for it—only beautiful. Isis had never seen anyone like him.

He had the most perfect nose she'd ever seen. His skin was so golden it was almost bronze. His cheekbones were high and his cheeks were a little hollow. He had lips like Johnny Depp's, sculpted and shapely, with a bit of a pout. His mouth held her fascinated for many long seconds and she knew instinctively that he was waiting for her to continue her study of his face, patiently, as though he had all the time in the world to do whatever it was he wanted to do with her.

"What do you want with me?" she asked again and was pleased that this time there was no tremor in her voice.

"Many things," he told her enigmatically, setting her gently away from him so that their faces were no longer a breath apart.

Isis didn't like that answer at all. "Who are you?" she asked, to cover up her discomfiture.

"I am Flare," he said.

Isis frowned. "What kind of a name is that?"

"My father named me thus after my first flame."

"I'm not even going to pretend to know what the hell you're talking about," she told him from behind pursed lips.

"Why do you dance nude before the eyes of strange men?" he asked suddenly, and there was a heat, an anger, in his voice that Isis couldn't ignore.

"Because it's good money," she told him simply.

"Do you need money so badly then?" He crossed his arms over his chest and Isis had a hard time ignoring the enormous bulge of his muscles.

"Everybody needs money badly," she scoffed. "Don't you?"

"We have no need for money here."

"'We'?" she asked. "Who is 'we'?"

He studied her for a long, silent moment. Isis was glad for the silence because his voice made her want to just jump his bones and have done with it. He seemed to come to some silent decision and motioned elegantly for her to take a seat. She did, simply because she didn't know what else to do, and he sat in a chair opposite her.

"I have been watching you," he said.

"Tell me something I don't know," she said flippantly.

He shook his head. "No. I have been watching you for two weeks now."

Isis choked on a gasp. "That's impossible. I would have known," she said disbelievingly.

"I thought so too. Your mind is open and I had to be very careful not to alert you. If not for last night, you would have never known I was there."

"Last night you killed a man," she accused in a hard voice.

"No. I killed a creature. What we call a Daemon. He was probably after *you*, actually, when I met up with him."

"You keep opening your mouth and saying words but they mean nothing to me," she scoffed. "Try talking in English."

"I thought I was," he said with a frown. "Perhaps my English is not that good. I don't know—I have never really tried it before."

"There you go again, making absolutely no sense. What do you mean you've never tried it before? You're speaking it aren't you—or trying to anyway. It would take a helluva lot of practice for you to speak so well if English is your second language."

"Actually I can speak any language on Earth. Somewhat," he said, his glowing eyes meeting hers, penetrating to her core. "I am sorry. I need to start over. I mean you no harm," he said soothingly, holding his hand out in a show of peace, which only served to remind her how he'd thrown the bouncers about like pixie sticks. "I vow it. I am pledged to protect you."

"Just tell me what the fuck is going on," she said breathlessly. His voice was getting to her again. "Start at the beginning or whatever. Enlighten me, if you're so eager to 'protect' me." She was proud that she managed to sound scathing and unafraid.

He studied her again with that still and powerful gaze of his. Then he shook his head and sighed. "I can tell by your pupil dilation and the rhythm of your breathing that you're still stressed," he said gently as if to not stress her any further. "You are tired. You don't sleep nearly enough, Isis. I think it best if we continue this conversation after you've had some rest."

"How do you know my name?" she demanded vehemently, forgetting for the moment that she was introduced on the stage each night for all to hear.

Flare rose in stoic silence and she followed. He went to the bedroom—God, even his most casual movements were sexy—and motioned toward the bed. "You can sleep there. I'll be close, just outside this door." He motioned to the sitting room entrance.

Isis hesitated. No way was she getting on that bed. Right? Damn. Her libido and her good judgment hadn't exactly reached an agreement on that yet. Not wanting to argue any further, she decided to trust him—whatever that meant—and approached the bed.

Flare grabbed her upper arm and turned her to face him. "You will never show your body to another man from this moment forth," he said firmly.

"Whatever," she snapped, hating being commanded by him. Because that was what it was—a command. And one he obviously fully expected her to obey. "I'll do whatever I want."

His grip tightened and he seemed to hesitate. Then he appeared to come to some decision and he jerked her to him. Before she could muster a complaint at being manhandled, Flare's lips slanted over hers and she lost all traces of any coherent thought.

The kiss burned her from head to toe. His lips were physically hot—all of him was, pressed up against her so domineeringly. Her breasts were crushed to his chest and he had dipped his head—he was so tall—his hair falling over them both like a curtain. It seemed to have a life all its own, tangling with hers so that they were joined even in the most basic of ways.

The pressure of Flare's lips demanded that she open her mouth. She did so and received the hot candy of his tongue as it stroked deeply beyond her lips to tangle and dance with her own. He had a flavor that was so unique she couldn't place it. He was spicy and sweet at the same time, like cinnamon or clove, and yet nothing at all like either.

Flare sucked her tongue into his mouth, inviting her to explore. She did, hesitantly at first, then with uncontrollable mounting desire. This was the first time she had ever willingly kissed a man and it was everything she could have hoped it would be and more.

Flare knew how to take total possession of her mouth and did so unhesitatingly.

The thick muscles of his arms crushed her to him so that their bodies touched from her breasts to her knees. Isis haltingly lifted her arms to pull him even closer when he grabbed them and forcefully put both her hands behind his neck. His hair was so soft, so silky, it sifted through her fingers deliciously as she clutched at him in desperation.

The heat of his kiss intensified and her mouth burned from it. Before she could stop him he had lifted her dress and his hands were on her bare breasts. Fear took hold and she tried to pull free from him, but he would not let her go. He ate at her mouth expertly, sensually, and she forgot her fear for the moment, enjoying the strange new sensations that were washing over and through her.

He backed her up to the massive bed. When Isis felt the mattress press against her bottom she panicked. Once more she tried to pull away and once more he would not let her. His fingers plucked delicately at her very erect nipples and her knees went liquid with desire. All thought of struggle was forgotten and Isis brazenly suckled on his tongue as it penetrated deep within her eager mouth, and her hands tightened around his neck, bringing him even closer.

As he kissed her, one of his hands left her breast and he reached up to take her hand. His fingers rested against her pulse and Isis knew with a certainty that it was deliberate. He wanted to feel her heart race. And oh how it *was* racing.

She pulled her hand away and put it back behind his head, fingers tangling in his luxurious hair as if they belonged there. Flare's lips nibbled at hers, more gently now, and his free hand slowly moved down to cup her sex. He had to feel how wet she was—her panties were no barrier to his touch. Flare stroked the lips of her pussy through the lace of her thong then unerringly zeroed in on her clit. His fingertips stroked and squeezed the nubbin of her clit until she was nearly crying with need.

He pushed her back onto the bed and she let him. She was mindless to anything but the amazing sensations that were flooding through her being. Flare's fingers caught in the lace of her panties and he ripped it from her body with a forceful tug that only inflamed her more. His fingers were slippery in her wetness, rubbing in all the right places, until they penetrated her, sliding deep and stretching her.

Panic assailed her once more. She jerked her mouth away from his and shrieked. She kicked him off her with one violent recoil of her legs and rolled swiftly off the bed, away from him.

"Don't come near me," she yelled as he approached her, hands outstretched, reaching for her. "Stay away."

"What have I done to make you fear me so?" he asked with a frown that did nothing to disguise the rampant desire still written in the lines of his face.

Isis took deep, gulping breaths and tried to slow the panicked beat of her heart. Flare put his hands down and studied her, his strange eyes missing nothing.

"You've been hurt by someone," he said with certainty.

Isis glared at him. "Shut up. Just go. Leave me alone," she demanded.

"I should not leave you like this," he said.

"I said leave me the fuck alone," she screamed, trembling fists clenching at her sides.

He watched her for another long, silent moment. Finally he nodded and headed for the door, careful to skirt around her so as not to cause alarm. "I will do as you wish," he said. "But you cannot ignore what is between us, Isis. Something has happened and we are both in this together."

"I can do whatever the hell I want," she panted. "*Leave*," she yelled with the last of her waning strength.

Flare did so, closing the door quietly behind him. Isis rushed to the other door that led out of the room and found it was locked, as she'd suspected it would be. She looked about the room in frustration, trying to keep her riotous emotions at bay and failing miserably.

With a last desperate breath she felt the tears begin to fall. She leaned against the door and when her knees gave out, slid to the floor. Isis cried silently, as she'd learned to do at a young age.

Her heart felt like it had been torn apart. After all these years she still couldn't accept a man's touch. It was embarrassing, alarming and hopeless. "Fuck," she whispered under her breath as the tears continued to fall onto her clasped hands held firmly in her lap to still their trembling.

Isis had long since thought she'd become numb to the pain. To the fear. But she had been wrong. Isis had cut herself off from any real human contact and now she was paying the price. There was no way she could have known that she would still react in such a way when a man touched her. She had avoided any scenario that would put her in that situation for just that reason.

The most beautiful man she'd ever seen had tried to seduce her and she had faltered, letting the fear consume her in a way she had vowed never to allow again. Isis banged her head back against the door and the tears continued to flow unchecked down her cheeks, dripping off her chin and jaw. She did it again, harder, and saw a burst of stars. Again and again she banged her head against the stone door until she felt strong arms scoop her up and away from her self-inflicted punishment.

"You are not well," Flare said gently. "I am sorry that I caused this pain in you."

Isis felt the tears continue to fall but refused to wipe them away. She'd never cried in front of anybody, but for some reason she didn't feel like hiding them from this man. "It's not your fault," she managed to say at last.

"It is," he said, laying her gently down upon the bed.

Her head hurt, but she welcomed the pain. Any other pain was welcome if it made her forget the pain in her heart. "No it isn't. I promise, it's not your fault. It's me," she painfully admitted.

"I have seen you. You cut yourself off from the world. You are totally alone. It hurts my heart to know that you suffer so."

Isis hid behind the fall of her hair but Flare would have nothing of it and he tucked her hair behind her ear with the gentlest touch.

"Don't worry about it," she said, fighting her tears. "I'll get over it."

"But what will happen when we come together again?" he asked softly.

Isis gritted her teeth. "We won't."

"We will," he insisted.

She realized that, in this situation, he was right. Wherever she was now, she was at his mercy. And what was more, she liked it. He was the first man she'd desired in so many years. And she *did* desire him. Fiercely. If she stayed near him it was inevitable that they would embrace again. What would she do then? Cower and let him have her, hating every moment? She couldn't have that—she had far too much pride. Besides, she didn't think Flare was the kind of man who would let his woman cower in bed.

"Tell me why you fear me," he said softly then smiled. "Besides the fact that I sort of kidnapped you," he joked lightly.

"You *did* kidnap me," she sniffed.

"Okay, so I did. But it was to protect you. No." He shook his head. "That's not true. I just could not bear the thought of other men seeing your body. I wanted to be the only one to see such a precious gift as the beauty of your bare skin."

Isis had never heard anything so beautiful and naked as his admission. Flare hid nothing of his feelings toward her and it made her desire him all the more.

Isis hated herself for her weakness. It wasn't that she didn't want Flare—God how she lusted after him, even after such a short time together—it was just that she couldn't get past her own tormented memories. They ate at her, drove her, warped her into something that wasn't entirely human but something baser, like a wounded beast caught in a trap. She was her own worst enemy and there was nothing she could think of that could change it.

Flare stroked his finger down her wet cheek. "Why do you weep so?"

"B-because I'm a failure," she admitted hesitantly.

"How are you a failure?" he asked.

"I can't be a woman. Not for you, not for anybody. Something's dead inside me and I can't do it. I just can't."

Flare stroked a hand over her hair. "You are strong, Isis. So strong. You do not even know the depths of your own will. You *are* a woman, Isis. And you are powerful, even though I can see that you think you are weak."

"Look at me." Isis held out her hands, the palms of which had bloody half moons tattooed into the flesh from her clenched nails digging mercilessly into the skin. "I'm a mess and all you did was kiss me and fondle me a little bit. God I'm pathetic." She put her hands on either side of her head and squeezed as if the motion would expel all of her demons.

Flare pulled her hands down gently but firmly. He held her hands in his and sat silently for a long moment. "You need rest."

"I can't sleep," she said with certainty.

Flare smiled and blew gently into her face.

Isis felt the darkness coming and welcomed it—a surcease from her horrifying pain. She was asleep before her head fell to the pillow. She didn't see Flare gently wipe the tears from her face. Nor did she see him cover her with a blanket with gentle care. She didn't see him leave the room, closing the door softly behind him. It didn't matter. She felt safe, *truly* safe, for the first time in her memory. And it was good.

Chapter Four

ಐ

Isis had no way of knowing what time it was when she woke up. There was no watch on her wrist—it hadn't been part of her costume—and there were no windows to see out of. She rubbed the sleep from her eyes and stretched, yawning uncontrollably. It felt like she'd slept for hours—she couldn't remember the last time she felt so well rested.

Rising from the bed, she smoothed her rumpled dress and approached the door that led to the sitting room. She put her ear to the door and listened, then promptly fell flat on her ass when Flare opened the door from the other side.

"I thought you would be awake," he said, holding out his hand to help her get back on her feet. Then he held out a steaming cup for her.

Thinking the drink was coffee, she took a healthy swig. The flavor of the drink—it definitely was not coffee—was like a cross between hot chocolate and vanilla milk. It was delicious. Addictive. Before she knew it, she had downed the whole thing. She wiped her mouth guiltily and handed the empty cup back to him with some chagrin.

"Would you like some more?" he asked.

"How did you make it without a kitchen?" she asked curiously.

"I am a bachelor. Several of the women provide me with meals and the like. Anything I need really."

"Because you're a bachelor?" she asked with incredulity.

"I am a warrior without a mate. It is how things are done here," he said simply.

"Where is here?" she asked, crossing her arms. "You make it sound like we're on a different planet."

Flare shook his head. "Not on a different planet. Simply far below the surface of the Earth."

"*What?*" she exclaimed.

"We are below the surface," he said again.

"So we're what, like, in a cave or something?" She frowned.

"No. It is difficult for me to explain—I have never had the need to. But what I am trying to tell you is that we are in a different dimension, far below the surface of the Earth. Very far. But not in a physical sense—if your people drilled to find this place they would never breach its boundaries."

"Like how far below are we?" she asked, eyes wide with shock.

"Hundreds of miles. Maybe more, I am not knowledgeable of such particulars. Needless to say we are far from the reach of the human world here."

"The *human* world?"

Flare took her hand and led her to one of the great chairs in the sitting room. "Sit. I have much to tell you and I am not certain where to start."

"Well, start at the beginning," she said in mounting exasperation and worry.

Flare went to his knees next to her, still holding her hand, fingers rubbing lightly over the beating of her pulse in her wrist. His eyes, when he met her gaze with his, were bright and golden, full of heat but also full of softer things. Things Isis didn't want to even think about just now.

"I am not human," he said, watching her closely as if to judge the reaction to his admission.

"You're not human?" she responded, mind blank with surprise. "Then what the hell are you?"

Flare grinned, showing off the straightest, whitest teeth she'd ever seen. "I am a Shikar warrior. I am part of an ancient race that has pledged to protect the human world from evil and destruction."

Isis had no idea how to react, so she said the first thing that came to mind. "Well, fuck, you guys are doing a terrible job." She could have kicked herself—there was no telling how Flare would react to her obviously disrespectful words.

"We try," he said. "But it is in your nature to destroy yourselves. We cannot change that."

"So what's your job as a warrior like?" She couldn't clear her thoughts to think of anything more intelligent to ask.

"I fight alone. Not all of us do," he explained. "I mainly hunt creatures like the one you saw me kill the other night."

"Creatures? What kind of creatures? You mean nonhuman, right?"

"Exactly. We call them Daemons. They feed on human suffering. They're..." He paused, looking for the right words. "They are sometimes large, sometimes small. Some of them are almost humanoid while others are nothing but horrific monsters. They too live below the surface of the Earth, but sometimes they make their way up to the surface and that is where I come in. I stop the monsters from killing innocents."

"How come I've never seen any proof of these so-called Daemons?" she asked suspiciously.

Flare sighed, as if the explanations were becoming tiresome. Isis thought he just wasn't used to talking so much—he struck her as kind of the silent, stoic type.

"There's plenty of proof out there to find," he admitted. "But your kind seems to look the other way when anything supernatural occurs around them. Our war is still a secret one simply because humans do not want to know about it."

Isis put a hand to her head and closed her eyes. When she opened them she met Flare's gaze and knew that he was telling her the truth. "How is this possible?" she whispered, desperately wanting to understand. "How could you have lived among us without our knowledge?"

"Humans always look the other way. It is the only explanation I have to give you," he said succinctly. "It is the only one I know."

Isis absorbed his words, silent for long moments. "What do I have to do with all this? You said that you'd been watching me for two weeks. Why would you do that?"

Flare studied her, wondering if she was strong enough for the full truth yet. She looked fragile, like glass that would splinter and break under too much pressure.

But there was a core of steel in her—he'd seen traces of it while watching her. She was stronger than she looked. He decided then that he would tell her everything and see how she reacted.

He watched her face closely when he answered. "You have a power. A psychic power that makes you a target for Daemons. Another group of Shikars discovered this—our spies, our Voyeurs. When we discovered it we realized that there had been increasing Daemon activity close to your dwelling and workplace. The Daemons were hunting you. I was assigned to protect you."

Isis looked nonplussed for a moment then Flare saw a mask come over her face, hiding all her emotions from him. Hiding all but what was in her most expressive hazel eyes. He could see her pain in there as well as her resolve not to show weakness in front of him. She was indeed stronger than she knew.

"Why you?" she asked in a hoarse voice.

"I am a strong warrior. I am a good Hunter. And I am a multiple Caste Incinerator—which means I can do many things to fight on your behalf, especially by creating and controlling flame. Our Elders thought I would be capable of offering you any assistance you might need."

"What do you care if I live or die? I'm a human. I have no ties to you." She blinked rapidly. Flare knew she was trying not to shout.

He decided to tell her the bald truth. "It is the Daemons we are concerned about. They are our enemy. If they were to capture you, feed on you, they would become stronger. We have to prevent such a thing at all costs. Whenever we find a human with this extrasensory perception that you possess, we protect them and in doing so we are fighting our enemy in the most effective way possible."

"I don't have any extrasensory whatever. I'm just a normal, quiet girl who struggles to make a living in a world that is very much against it."

Flare wondered if she believed her own words. He had been assured that she was indeed a strong psychic and he trusted his sources and his own perception. After watching her for two weeks he knew that there was something special about her, something extra that so few other humans possessed. He wondered if he were to test her, would she rise to the challenge and discover the strength within herself?

"Wait a minute," she said suddenly. "Just how many so-called psychics are there?"

"We don't know. We've only come across a handful in thousands of years of existence. You're unique in a very special way, a very unlikely way. One day you will discover your power. It is inevitable," he told her gently.

Isis stared off into space. Flare had noticed her doing this many times before, distancing herself from her surroundings, from her present situation. Seeking refuge within the still world of her mind. He waited patiently for her to come to terms with what he had told her thus far. If Isis needed anything it was patience, and luckily he had great reserves of it.

But his patience would not last forever. He knew that. For now he would go at her pace, guide her to the truth with a gentle hand and hopefully find out why she went berserk when he'd touched her the previous night.

That more than anything, even his sworn duty as a warrior, was what concerned him now.

He wanted her. Fiercely. He had known from the first few days of watching her that he wanted her. And not for just one night of pleasure, but for many. Flare didn't know how the Elders would react to his claim on this woman—for he *would* claim her—and he didn't care. He would have her. Flare could settle for nothing less.

But there was something badly damaged inside of her. He had seen it from afar and now firsthand. Something horrible had happened to her, he was certain of it. She had no love for herself. In fact, it seemed that she hated herself most of the time. Flare wanted to know why and he wanted to fix it for her. Now. But he knew it would take time before she would open up to him. He was willing to wait—but only for so long—before he took things into his own hands.

Isis seemed to come back to herself with a start. She frowned and met his gaze with her own. "When will you take me back?"

Flare thought for a moment. He wanted to keep her here, but he knew for certain that the Elders would frown on him keeping a woman confined to his quarters, especially one as precious as this. He would have to take her back. For now.

"I'll take you back whenever you want. But I will never leave you, not so long as you have need of me."

"So you'll baby-sit me," she scoffed. "I don't like knowing you'll be spying on me."

"I won't be spying exactly," he smiled wryly. "But I *will* be watching over you."

"You can't come into the club and carry me off again like that. Ever." She ran a hand through her hair in obvious frustration. "I don't even have a clue how I'm going to explain what happened to my boss."

Flare gritted his teeth and anger made the heat bake off him in waves. He tamped down on his anger, not wanting to alarm her. "I don't want you working there anymore," he told her honestly.

"I have to," she told him. "The money is good and I need it to survive. It's a very easy way to make a lot of money really fast."

"I do not like knowing that other men are looking upon your bare flesh." He rose suddenly and went to retrieve a large stone box from one of his shelves.

Isis gasped to see what was in the box. When he opened it, dozens of slips of paper fell out. It was jam-packed with money—all kinds of money from all over the world. He rummaged through the paper money as if it meant nothing to him and retrieved a very thick wad of green bills.

"You must take this and promise me that you will no longer bare yourself before strangers." He handed her the wad of hundred-dollar bills. There had to be a good two hundred of them. Twenty thousand dollars in the palm of her hand. And Flare hadn't even hesitated to give it to her.

"Is it enough?" he asked hopefully.

Isis swallowed hard. She knew it would be hard to return to the club and explain away the fantastical events that had occurred. It might be impossible. She sighed and made her decision. "You don't need this money?"

"No," he admitted easily.

"Then I'll consider it your karmic obligation for ruining my job," she said flippantly.

"I can get you more if you need it. As much as you want," he told her.

Isis felt her eyes go wide with surprise. "Just how do you get this money?" she asked. "I'm not going to go to jail or anything if I try to spend it?"

"The Elders supply us with funds in case we have need of it in the Territories."

"The Territories?" She frowned.

"It's what we call the surface world. It is but a small Territory of the world we know. As for the money, you needn't worry that it will land you in legal trouble. And we have endless supplies of it. It would be nothing for me to supply you with an equal amount of money every week if need be."

Isis tried to take it all in. Then her naturally suspicious nature reared its ugly head. "Why are you doing this?"

Flare took her hand once more in his. Again he let his fingers caress her pulse, and she knew it was his way of judging her mood by the pace of her beating heart.

His gaze met hers and it was as though flames flickered within his eyes. "I do this because I do not want you to display your body before anyone but me. The money is such a small thing for me. Please, I beg you, take the funds I offer and give up your line of work. You must stop. I cannot bear it." His fingers stroked her palms with the gentlest of touches but his voice was tortured and hurt.

The raw honesty in his voice humbled her. Flare was so unafraid to tell her his feelings that it made her feel like she was hiding behind a mask. She wished she could be so honest, so open, but she'd long ago learned that such a thing was dangerous in the extreme. To let someone know you cared was to give them a weapon to use against you. And Isis had vowed never to care for anyone again.

She steeled her heart. "I'll do whatever I damn well please and there's nothing you can do about it." She hated herself for the words that came out of her mouth, but the ever-present pain in her heart drove her emotions and she couldn't stop. She didn't want to strip. She had never wanted to strip. But it had been so easy after she'd done it once and then again, and again. Here was her chance to stop and never have to worry about money again and she was turning it down in the rudest way possible. Isis could have kicked herself for her foolish pride, but it was too late. She'd already made her decision. She couldn't let Flare take care of her like a man might provide for his mistress or prostitute. Doing that would be far worse than stripping in her eyes.

Flare's grip on her hand tightened and his flesh grew alarmingly hot. "I will not let you do it. If need be, I will carry you out of that club every night as I did last night. I care not that your people will see me for what I am—an Incinerator, a Shikar—I care only that you stop this line of work."

Isis tried to pull her hand back but he wouldn't let go and only held it tighter, his skin nearly singeing hers it had grown so hot. "You can't stop me," she heard herself say and immediately she knew it was the wrong thing to say to him.

"You give me little choice," he said tightly. "You know I could keep you here, against your will, forever if I so choose to."

"You wouldn't," she said with a show of confidence she did not feel.

"I won't let you keep doing this."

"You have no choice in the matter," she told him plainly. "Now," she said more gently, "take me home."

Flare stood swiftly and jerked her to her feet. She fell, off balance, against him. One of his hands held her arm with easy strength and the other tangled in the hair at the nape of her neck. Isis saw what he meant to do and there was no fight in her. She wanted it as much as he did. Maybe even more.

The heat of his lips on hers was intense. She gasped, opening her mouth and accepting his tongue. He kissed her forcefully, bending her to his will with nothing but the strength of their combined passion. Heat wafted off him in waves and she instinctively knew this was no simple kiss of seduction, but a forceful reminder of who had the upper hand in this bizarre situation she found herself in.

His kiss ended as abruptly as it had begun and she nearly fell against him as she fought to keep kissing him. They broke apart, both breathless and shaken. "I'll take you home," he said and reached for her once again.

Chapter Five

ഇ

The world fell away, the great stone chamber disappearing, and she felt that strange sensation of flying at high speed, almost as if she were caught in the path of a hurricane. Seconds passed — years could have passed and she wouldn't be the wiser — as she clung to him with her eyes shut tight. Then she felt the ground beneath her feet once more and when she opened her eyes she saw that she was at The Pink Pit, beside her car, in the dead of night.

"Neat trick. But I don't have my keys."

Flare disappeared. Isis, startled, looked around but saw nothing out of the ordinary. The man had simply vanished before her eyes. A second later he reappeared and handed over her purse. She took it, not even wanting to know how he'd gotten the thing, and automatically dug for her car keys.

"Okay," she said slowly, dragging the word out. Isis shook her head as if to clear it. "Get in," she said finally, unlocking the car's doors with a press of a button on her key.

"Will you try to dance tonight?" he asked.

Isis heard the key word in his question. "Try". He still meant to stop her from doing her job. She admired his tenacity. She shook her head again. "I'm not scheduled for tonight," she told him simply as she cranked the car and pulled away from the nearly empty parking lot.

"God, I wonder what time it is," she mused aloud. The night was deep and dark, well underway, but how far?

"It's five and a half hours until sunup," Flare told her promptly.

"How do you know that?" She glanced at him for a second then resumed looking at the road before her.

"I can feel the sun."

"Right now? In the dead of night?" Isis asked, incredulous. This magic man was so full of surprises that she wasn't sure her heart could take much more.

"Shikars cannot stand the sun. Well, *most* cannot," Flare quickly rectified. "Its rays are too strong and it burns our skin."

"So you won't be watching me by day, only by night?" she exclaimed, nonplussed.

"You won't need protection by day," he told her gently. "The Daemons can only come out by night. You need not fear that I would ever willingly place you in danger." Flare's voice was soothing, reassuring, calming to her frayed nerves.

Isis managed a chuckle. "Well, that's a relief."

"I mean what I say." His voice was now diamond hard.

Isis glanced at him, meeting his incredible gaze with her own for a few short seconds before she was forced to focus once more on the road. "I know you mean it," she said softly. "And I am grateful."

"I do not require your gratitude."

"What do you require then?" she shot back.

"I require you to stop hurting so much. Whatever it is that has broken you, we can overcome it together if you would just let me champion you." Flare's words were flat and matter of fact, as if he truly believed in them.

But Isis knew better. Nothing could overcome her demons. Nothing and no one but herself, and she was already so tired of fighting them that she was truly, spiritually exhausted. "You wouldn't understand," she told him finally.

"I would," he argued.

"Look," she began, "I don't want to talk about it. I'm not broken so don't think you need to try to fix me."

"But you *are* wounded," he insisted. "Simply tell me who wounded you and I will stamp them out utterly."

Isis believed him. "You don't have to worry about me. I can take care of myself."

"Last night you could not take care of yourself," he reminded her mercilessly.

Taking a deep calming breath, she focused intently on the feel of the road beneath her tires. "I can't tell you," she said. "I've only told one other person and she couldn't believe me. You wouldn't understand, okay? I don't even understand it. Let's just leave it at that."

"I will leave it for now. I can see how it upsets you. But we will soon cross a bridge that will lead to our joining, and I won't have you frightened of my touch."

"I'm not afraid," she lied.

"Then stop this car and join with me now."

Isis laughed, she just couldn't help herself. "I will not have sex with you in my car. There isn't enough room to maneuver anyway."

"I'll manage," he insisted.

"I'll bet you would," Isis said with a smile. She tried hard to ignore the rising passion the sound of his voice inspired in her. And when he said such romantic things her knees went weak and her heart melted—but she was determined not to let her emotions overcome her. That would get her nowhere.

Nowhere but in his arms.

And why was she so afraid of that—for she was indeed afraid. Her past was over and done with. She should have jumped this warrior's bones several times over by now. He was the sexiest being she'd ever seen and everything about him was a sort of sensual seduction, entrancing her, addicting her to him.

All this and she'd only known him for a day. She felt like a fool, but there was no way she could ignore her attraction. Flare was just so…delicious. Isis could hardly stand it. She was getting wet just listening to him talk for Christ's sake. It was overwhelming to think how she would react with him inside her. And she wanted that— she wanted to join with him. But the question was…*could* she?

Later, after they'd pulled into her driveway, Flare raised her hand to his lips and kissed it. He didn't say anything, just released her hand and got out of the car without even glancing her way. He came around to her side of the car and gallantly opened the door for her, yet still he held his silence. Isis wondered what he was thinking as she followed him to her front door.

Flare was thinking of how he could seduce her into opening her heart to him. He didn't just want her body — he wanted all of her. He was breathless with desire. He wanted to be a part of her thoughts always, and he wanted to be physically and spiritually one with her as often as possible. Flare's heart beat a heavy staccato in his breast — it raced every time he looked at Isis. His cock was hard and heavy in his pants, and he knew that if Isis were to just glance down she'd see how much he needed her. He wouldn't hide his body's reaction to her though. She needed to become accustomed to his desire, for he knew it would never wane, only grow stronger with each passing heartbeat.

Something itched at the back of his mind and he was suddenly alert to his surroundings, not just the fascinating woman at his side. This was a familiar feeling — and it didn't bode well.

Isis rummaged to find her house key. Flare pushed her aside and forced her door open with nothing but the palm of his hand against the wood. He left black, singed fingerprints behind in the wood. "Get in," he told her, pushing her inside with a strength that frightened her. The air around her was suddenly boiling hot.

"What's going on —"

"Get inside. *Now.*" He pulled the door shut on her without waiting for her acquiescence.

Isis stamped her foot in frustration. "Fine," she called out, knowing he would hear her. "I'll just stay here then. Damn it."

* * * * *

Flare felt the dangerous threat that hung in the air like a palpable thing and knew with certainty that a Daemon was near. But where? Daemons were tricky bastards, having mastered the art of Traveling in recent years. They could disappear and reappear at will, just as he could. Though their numbers were dwindling, those that survived the Shikars' justice were growing stronger with each passing day and Flare knew the one he was about to face was a nasty bugger. He could feel it.

Looking around carefully, he stepped out into the open, welcoming an attack. Flare was a multiple Caste Shikar. He could Travel, Incinerate, use his Foils and Hunt almost as well as those of the Hunter Caste. Mostly he was an Incinerator, for he much preferred to fight with flame and his fire-making abilities were legendary among his people, second only to the warrior named Cinder. He let a flame lick up his arm, not feeling its burn in the least, illuminating the impenetrable darkness around him. "Come forward and meet me, vile sub-creature," he called out, hoping to goad his adversary out of its hiding place.

Shocked when three Daemons stepped out from the border of trees, Flare steeled himself for the battle ahead. It had been so long since he'd seen a pod of Daemons—not since the great battle at the Gates—and he knew then that Isis must be powerful indeed for the creatures to make such a valiant effort to claim her.

He let the flame lick up his arm and form a halo about his head. He marched with long strides toward his enemies, carefully studying them to see how they were going to react in this battle. Soon his whole body was ablaze with golden light as he let the Daemons see the strength of his power. Fiery red Foils shot out from his knuckles like swords, giving him over two feet of razor-sharp, smoldering claws with which to combat his prey.

All three of the Daemons turned and fled back into the trees. Flare Traveled, disappearing from his station in the yard and reappearing in the path of the fleeing beasts. The Daemons snarled and halted, then without warning they all struck at once, coming at him from all directions.

Flare let the flames of his power consume him. He used all of his brute strength to stand against their attack. He jumped several feet into the air and came down with his Foils at the ready, cutting one creature completely in half with one blow and, with a powerful strike of his hands, severely wounding the other two. Still the creatures would not stop in their struggle, and Flare knew they would fight until the very last moment when he had their hearts aflame in his hand.

Isis watched this from a window, seeing Flare light up the night like a Roman candle as he—there was no other word for it—*stalked* up to three dark figures just beyond the line of trees around her house. The flames around him illuminated the dark night, and bright, red-hot blades seemed to shoot forth from his hands, giving him claws. Then he flew straight into the air, coming down with all of his power. Though he was large and muscular he danced easily around his adversaries and landed several more blows, his movements unbelievably graceful. She could no longer see much of the three Daemons—if that was indeed what they were—as Flare's bright flames grew ever more intense, but she could tell that he was deadly serious in his mission to protect her.

He would not stop until the threat to her was finished. The Daemons didn't stand a chance.

A sound behind her startled her and she turned.

Isis caught her breath painfully and swallowed a cry.

She was face-to-face with a seven-foot, three-hundred-pound monster. There was no other word for what this being was — Daemon, whatever, she didn't care, it was a *monster* plain and simple. Its face was a mess of mangled parts, if it could be called a face. Its body was thick and black and it looked like it was covered in goo. It had overly long arms and spikes from shoulders to wrists. Its legs were shaped like a dog's — they looked backward — and its feet were massive claws that dug grooves into the wood of her living room floor.

"You are one ugly motherfucker," she whispered, more to herself than to the beast overshadowing her. It grunted and said something in gibberish she couldn't understand. The sound of its voice was like the sound someone would make if they raked their fingers across a rusty car door. She screamed despite herself, truly horrified by the monster's voice, and darted around the hulking brute, racing deeper into her house, heading for the back door.

The horrible, rending feel of her flesh being torn washed over her back. She actually felt the beast's claws penetrate her flesh, one by one, like ten-inch nails, and she screamed uncontrollably as it ravaged her back with but one swipe of its hand. The pain was immediate and intense. She stumbled but forced herself to keep running despite the overwhelming, mind-blowing agony gouged into the skin of her back. Isis knew that if she let the monster get close again it would do far worse than claw her back.

She nearly threw herself out the back door but she didn't stop there. Isis sprinted full out, running as fast as she could, not heading in any specific direction, just *away* from the thing that dogged her heels.

It was almost as if she could feel the breath of the beast on the back of her neck. She screamed again and ran harder, until her tortured flesh screamed in agony. Within seconds she made it to the border of trees. She ran into the forest, not even bothering to avoid the branches that smacked her in the face and tore at her hair and clothing. Nothing mattered now, no pain, no fear, no weariness. The only thing that mattered was getting away from this monster.

Isis ran deep into the forest. She ran until her sides felt like they were sliced open with razors and her lungs ached as if she weren't breathing oxygen, but smoke. Hot, thickly cloying smoke that choked her painfully. Her mouth was dry and her face hurt from all the branches she was running into, and the blood was pounding heavily in her head. She heard a rumbling behind her, then a shrieking roar like the sound of a thousand dying souls. The sound terrified her even more than the sight of the thing, turning her overheated blood to ice in her fiercely pumping veins as she flew blindly through the trees.

Her foot caught painfully on an exposed root and she fell, hitting her chin hard on a stone and scraping her palms on the ground so that they stung and bled. She glanced back and shrieked as the monster came for her, claws outstretched.

Something snapped inside her. She had only felt such a strange sensation one other time in her life. It was as if something dark and deadly had reared its head inside of her mind and heart. Isis felt swollen with a sudden and fierce rage and there was no outlet—but for the Daemon.

With a wild cry she flew to her feet and launched herself at the monster. Striking out with her fist, with a power that was far beyond what any human should possess, she obliterated the monster's hellish face. Bone and sinew crunched as her fist actually sank into a crater she had created with the force of her blow.

The monster fell at her feet and she was on him, her unbelievable rage making her brave beyond anything she could have imagined. She doubled her fists and brought them down over her head, striking the beast squarely in the heart. Her hands sank into flesh and goo, and hot, black blood spurted in every direction. She went nearly elbow deep into the chest cavity and felt around in the slime and gristle for the Daemon's beating heart.

"Isis!"

She heard Flare call out to her but she was mindless and unable to answer him with anything but a roar of pure, hot anger.

Thick and heavy, like a living stone, the heart seemed to fall into her hands as if by magic. She jerked back, lifting the Daemon with the force of her movement, and pulled the heart free from its ravaged rib cage. The heart beat a fast staccato in her hand and she screamed in rage and despair, tearing the heart asunder. When she did so, the giant Daemon went limp beneath her, completely lifeless.

But she couldn't stop what she had unleashed. Isis beat at the body over and over, her fists sinking deep into flesh and sinew with each powerful strike. She was covered from head to knees in thick, black blood and she stank of the monster—like rotting flesh and brimstone—but still she could not stop fighting. She realized that she was shrieking uncontrollably, her body shaking so hard that her teeth rattled. And though she wanted to, still she could not stop.

"Baby. Baby...it's all right."

She heard Flare's words as if from miles away. She felt strong yet gentle arms come around her and pull her from the ravaged carcass, but she fought with all her might not to let go of her hold on the creature. Flare would not be deterred however, and he finally wrenched her away, turning her in his arms so that she didn't have to see the horror of what she had done. He held her tight as she reflexively fought to be free from him—striking him with blows that would have crippled a human. He took her punishment, all the while talking in a low, soothing voice to try to reach her higher consciousness.

"Shhh. It's over now, baby. You can stop fighting," he murmured into her hair as he cradled her to him despite her waning struggles. "It's dead. It's gone."

Isis fell to her knees, put her head in her hands and screamed. It was a long, tortured sound. She couldn't believe the sound came from within her, but it went on and on endlessly, and she couldn't stop it.

Eventually, of course, she ran out of breath. She sat in the dirt and leaves and panted heavily. Flare bent down next to her and put his hands on either side of her head. He made her look at him and she tried hard to focus on his face with anger-blurred vision.

"Tamp down on your power, Isis. Use your will. The rage will pass."

She took deep breaths and did as he commanded. With a resolve she didn't know she was capable of, she pushed the anger away. It took a physical effort—her hands pushing against her wildly beating heart—and it exhausted her, but she did it. The fiery rage cooled until it was no more than a fly buzzing in the bright light of her mind, and she was once more capable of rational thought and intelligible speech.

Isis looked up at him bemusedly. "He hurt me," she said, unable to think of anything more intelligent at the moment.

Flare was immediately concerned. "Where did he hurt you?" he asked with rushed words.

Her hand trembled as she reached behind her to feel the ravaged flesh of her back. The pain, gone during her trip to psycho land, came back with a vengeance and she cried out before she could stop herself. "My back," she told him, turning so that he could see her wounds. "The bastard cut me really deep."

Flare studied her wounds. "I can heal these," he reassured her. "I will steal the pain away, Isis. I promise." He jerked the cloth of her dress down around her waist and laid his hands on her naked, torn flesh, palms flat against the bloodied plains of her back. Searing heat burned her and she yelped then gritted her teeth to prevent any other sound from escaping and betraying her anguish.

The heat soon abated and instantly her back felt better. Breathing a heavy sigh of sweet relief, she relaxed and let him work his magic. The agony of her rent flesh faded until there was nothing left but soothing heat in its place. It took only minutes, but it felt more like hours before her suffering ended. But it *did* end—thanks to Flare's amazing, healing touch.

He took her hands in his and stroked his fingertips over her ragged, bleeding palms. Isis actually witnessed the tiny lacerations closing, leaving only the traces of her spilt blood behind. She showed him the gash on her chin and he touched her there as well, warming her from head to toe with the enormous heat baking off his skin, and the pain was gone as if it had never been there.

"What the fuck just happened here?" she panted.

"I told you that you had power within you. This has been but a taste of that strength. You need to be taught to control it, to hone and perfect it so that it can be used as a weapon at any time. We'll practice that later."

Isis looked at him, eating him up with her eyes. She had never been so happy to see anyone in her life. She threw herself at him and he caught her easily, as if he'd been waiting for her to do just that. Isis wrapped her arms around his neck and pulled his mouth down to hers.

The burn of his lips on hers was almost painful—he was just so hot. Literally. But Isis welcomed that heat and returned it with a passion she hadn't known she was capable of, plunging her tongue into his sweet mouth to taste and tease.

Flare put his hands gently on either side of her face and tilted it just so, so that his lips could slant over hers as he took control of the kiss. He ravaged her mouth, but his hands were so soft, as if he was mindful of his own strength so as not to hurt her. Their hair ruffled in a small breeze, tangling, binding them together. Flare's scent—spicy and woodsy—intoxicated her so that she grew dizzy and fell weakly against his chest, kissing him even more deeply.

Her heart beat a wild tattoo in her chest and her breath came in short gasps. Her breasts, still bared to the air with her dress rumpled at her waist, ached and felt heavy. Her nipples felt like little stones on the crest of her breasts, hard and thick and tight. A feeling like being shocked with electricity washed from the top of her head straight to her pussy, and she was immediately wet and ready for him in a way she had never been ready for any other man before.

They were covered in evidence of their battles but neither cared. Flare's hands left her face and moved to fist in the hair that spilled down the middle of her back, pulling her so close that she had to struggle to breathe. But it was all right. She had no fear, no anxiety—only pure need. Isis kissed him as she'd never kissed another, freely and eagerly putting all of her passion and mounting desire into the caress of fire in his lips on hers.

A strong breeze blew dry, fallen leaves about them, as if the wind felt their emotion and was responding in kind. They parted, both panting, with locked gazes and clasped hands.

"We need to get clean," he told her softly, tucking a lock of hair behind her hair.

"Yes," she agreed, finally looking down at herself. She was covered in blood and gore—not at all romantic.

Still, it somehow didn't matter. Isis knew that she would accept Flare on any terms, no matter the situation. She had bonded fast to him, something she had never experienced, and she wanted nothing more than to solidify their growing connection to each other.

Flare surged to his feet and lifted her hand to help her rise beside him. He took one look at the fallen body of the Daemon, as if he'd almost forgotten it was there. He winked at Isis, kissed his left index finger, pointed it at the Daemon and a stream of unchecked fire exploded from his fingertip, turning the body of the monster to ash in a matter of seconds. The stream of fire stopped as swiftly as it had begun and Flare blew on the tip of his finger so that a tiny stream of smoke rose up into the air.

"Let's go get washed up."

He tucked her protectively beneath his arm, clutching her close to his side in an awkward sort of hug. Isis held the tattered dress to her body. Even though she was far beyond caring about her nudity, it just seemed like the right thing to do. She fell into step beside him, matched her stride to his much longer one and leaned against him, quaffing from his seemingly endless well of strength.

They slowly walked back to the house by the light of the moon through the trees, hands clasped tight, fingers entwined and two hearts beating as one.

Chapter Six

❧

Isis wanted to share the shower with him. But Flare would have none of it.

"You need a soft bed beneath you when you are beneath me," he said arrogantly. "I won't take you for the first time in the shower. You deserve better."

As far as excuses went, it was perfect. Isis took the first shower, taking twice as long as she normally would have because it was nearly impossible to get all the blood off. It had dried to a hard, tar-like substance on her skin and it took several minutes of vigorous scrubbing to rid herself of the muck. When she was done, her skin was a rosy pink from head to toe. She grabbed a thick towel from the bar beside the shower and threw her heavy fall of wet hair over her shoulder, wrapping the towel around her body securely.

When she stepped from the bathroom Flare was right there waiting for her, and from the heated look in his unique golden eyes, she knew he was pleased with her freshly scrubbed face. She could understand why. Before her shower the makeup she'd put on the night before had been smeared all over her face, giving her an almost haggard look. Isis was happy to rid her skin of the cosmetics and doubly happy to see Flare's reaction to her fresh new look.

Flare's shower took a while as well, for he too had been covered in the filth of his battles. When he stepped from the bathroom with a towel draped around his waist, Isis was sitting at her dressing table, gazing into a mirror as she parted her hair evenly. Flare came up behind her and put his hands on her shoulders. Isis looked up at him in the mirror, seeing how tall and dark he looked compared to her, standing so strong and still behind her.

His hair was wet and blue-black, falling far down his back. His jaw was square and strong, his nose straight and noble, his pouting lips a naturally rosy hue. The smooth muscles of his chest were massive, like a bodybuilder's might have been. He had a toned six-pack on his midsection, his waist tapering down to lean hips then flaring out again at the thick musculature of his thighs. The muscles in his arms were the same—his upper arms were so thick she wouldn't have been able to put both hands around them had she tried. He was a magnificent specimen of a male, no matter his species.

Their gazes met and held. Desire was naked in their eyes. Isis stood up from her station at the table and turned to him. With trembling hands, she unknotted her robe and let it fall to the floor. The look of heat within his eyes emboldened her. She stepped closer to him and put her arms around his neck.

"Kiss me," she whispered, tilting her head back to receive the soft, too gentle press of his lips.

Isis wanted more. She used her tongue to open Flare's mouth and taste him. He gave her his tongue and she suckled on it gently. Their teeth clicked together and that sensation made them both clutch tighter to each other. Flare fisted one hand in the hair at the middle of her back and used the other to cup her neck.

There was a moment when Isis was fully aware of just how easily Flare could kill her were he to tighten his hand around her neck. But the thought did not bring the expected fear and anxiety. She knew instinctively, the knowledge so strong it flowed through her veins, that he would never hurt her. And he would die to protect her.

That knowledge was heady, exponentially increasing her need, and she moaned into his mouth. He swallowed the sound and brought her tighter to him. The heavy, hard press of his cock was alarming, but only for a brief moment. And it wasn't alarming for the reasons she might have been accustomed to. It was alarming because he was so incredibly huge.

The feel of his naked skin against her breasts stole her breath away. She tingled from head to toe, especially in her lips, breasts and pussy. It was as if her whole body could feel his touch, as if he had a thousand hands instead of two.

The temperature of the room had risen several degrees and Flare's skin was growing hotter with each passing second. But the heat did not hurt her. Instead it embraced her, making her feel safe and wanted. Her head swam dizzily, as if she was drunk, and she gasped for breath. Flare gave her his own, filling her with his heat from deep within, making her skin burn deliciously all over.

Her hands tangled in the hair at the nape of his neck and she held him closer. She broke away from his lips and traced her own over his eyes, nose and cheeks. His skin was so smooth. She dotted kisses all over him, not missing an inch of his beautiful face. Flare growled and put both hands on either side of her head to hold her still as he reclaimed her mouth with his once again.

All these sensations and all they had done was kiss. The thought of going further enflamed her senses and her hands frantically clutched at him.

Flare's lips gentled against hers. "There's no rush, baby," he murmured into her lips. "Slow down."

She tried, she really did, but her body was rampant with want and need. It was a heady feeling. Isis did something she'd never thought she'd do in a million years. She climbed him like she would the pole at the club and wrapped her legs around his waist to hold herself up. Flare's hands went to cup her bottom and she tightened her arms around his neck, licking his lips hungrily.

Their mouths fused together. And the feel of his terry-cloth-covered, rock-hard cock between her legs nearly made her come right then and there. His fingers nearly singed the flesh of her ass, but the near-pain of his touch only spurred her on. Isis began to squeeze his waist, moving up and down against his cock. Flare growled and lifted her higher, holding her tight to still her movements.

But Isis was lost in a raging passion she had never experienced before. She demanded to feel him and wiggled her bottom back down so that Flare's cock was once again cradled by her wet, aching pussy. Flare stubbornly lifted her again and broke away from their kiss. He bent his head before she could pull him back, fast as a striking cobra, and took nearly her whole left breast into his super-heated mouth.

Isis cried out, a low, broken sound that only served to further enflame them both. Flare's teeth scraped over the swell of her breast. He pulled back slowly, sensually, until only her long, hard nipple was in his mouth. The lick of flame that was his tongue made her entire body clench with need as it flicked back and forth over her nipple. Isis' head fell back, her long hair spilling down almost to the floor as she arched higher into this new, wicked embrace.

Flare was lost to his passion just as Isis was. A raging demon, riding him hard, demanded that he take her then and there.

But there was a catch that Flare was holding fast to in his passion-clouded mind.

He couldn't have unprotected sex with her. Not yet at least. He needed her love first, her whole heart, for such a thing to happen. He wouldn't put her in any such danger, not ever. It would take an act of pure love—on both their parts—to see her through their exchange of fluids.

The feel of her legs wrapped around his waist nearly brought him to his knees. Her arms were like cloying vines, holding him impossibly close to her. Her nipple tasted like candy and its texture tickled his tongue. Flare licked her over and over again and sucked her hard between his nibbling teeth. He tore another cry from her and he drank the sound in like a man dying of thirst. There was nothing more beautiful, more moving, than Isis in her full passion. He felt humbled by the power of their desire. Nothing had ever come close to this, not in all his two hundred years of life.

The thud of his heart sounded in his ears. There was a physical ache there, in his chest, and he knew with certainty he'd never known before that he loved this woman. Things for him had gone far beyond mere desire. She'd touched his heart, his soul, and she'd changed his life forever.

He wanted to hold her tight and steal her pain away. Though she was strong and valiant and brave, there was an endless sense of suffering about her. Flare knew someone had hurt her. Someone she had cared about. The thought made his body flare up several degrees and he tamped down on his power to keep from hurting Isis. He didn't like the thought of her caring for anybody but him.

And their future children, of course.

There was no way he could let her go now. Not after basking in the glow of her natural sensuality. If he had to, he would *make* her love him. He could accept no less from her. Her life had been in his care for two weeks and he'd learned much about her in that time. Isis was alone — utterly. She had no friends, no lovers, no one. She was often quiet, introspective. There was an adorable tendency in her to daydream. Her bravery was evident in the way she took care of herself and kept away from attachments of any sort. She wasn't afraid to be lonesome — in fact, she welcomed it.

Flare knew with a certainty that she would make a magnificent lover. She was like liquid fire in his arms. And all the pent-up passion she'd stowed away over the years had come out like a violent storm between them.

Her skin was so soft, so tender. She was smooth all over — even her pussy was hairless and smooth, he'd noticed. He would have liked to see her red hair there between her legs. But the thought of being able to kiss her bare skin made up for that and more. None of his past lovers had been without hair between their legs and he was looking forward to the new sensation of Isis' bald cunt wrapped tight around his cock.

These thoughts and more made him breathless with desire. He couldn't hold back anymore. He took her to the bed and lowered her onto it. She kept her legs wrapped tight around his waist. He reached between them and removed the towel that covered him.

Isis looked down and gasped. Jesus Christ the man was ginormous! He had to be at least eleven inches long and over two inches thick. The thickness of him surprised her more than the length. But, then again, Flare was a big, strong man—all over. She should have expected it—yet the reality was far more powerful than anything she could have imagined. Isis was intimidated for a moment, but only a moment. There was a certainty in her that this was right, that this was clean and pure and honest. And she knew Flare would make sure she was ready for his impalement. She let herself sink into the pleasure of being in Flare's arms, letting all her fears and misgivings go.

Flare's lips moved from breast to breast, as if he couldn't decide which one was his favorite, and soon she was writhing beneath him. He'd laid her down so that her bottom was only just supported by the edge of the mattress and he sank to his knees by the bed to fit better against her. The naked feel of his cock in the wet channel of her spread legs made her give a short scream of excitement that seemed to drive Flare wild.

His kisses became more forceful. The darkness of his head moved down her as he pressed hot, hard kisses to her stomach. Then he seemed to grasp the reins of his control once more and he gentled his caress, lightly tracing his tongue up and down the middle of her body, nipping at her delicate skin with his lip.

Letting her hands fall away from his neck, she put them over her head and arched into his touch. His hands stroked her from hips to wrist, leaving a wake of fiery heat behind. He repeated the caress and she moaned. The tips of his fingers lingered on her wrists, feeling for the beating of her pulse, and Isis knew he was checking to see how aroused she was—as if the wetness of her body wasn't evidence enough. He released her and Flare held her hips still as he bent lower and before she knew how to react, his lips and tongue were on her pussy.

Her hips nearly bucked him away. Isis cried out, long and low and loud, the sound echoing in both their ears. Flare's hands pushed her legs impossibly wide and he licked her from clit to anus. Isis was mindless, out of control, and more than eager to experience more of his most wicked kiss. He licked her again, his saliva mixing with her own juices, making her so slippery that his tongue met no resistance when it finally penetrated her.

Isis shrieked and came up off the bed. But he stayed with her, plunging his tongue deep within her over and over again, his hands never leaving the tender flesh of her inner thighs as he forced her legs to stay open for him. Isis put her hands in his silky hair, fisting them there as she strained against him eagerly. Her entire body shook with her trembling and her heart felt like it would fly up into her throat.

"Please," she begged in a ragged voice, not knowing what she was begging for but begging for it all the same. "Oh God, Flare, *please, please, please!*" Her head thrashed back and forth on the bed, her hair tangling wildly around her flushed face. Flare thrust his tongue into her one last time, reaching impossibly deep inside of her.

One of his long, strong fingers thrust into her to replace his tongue and it was such a new and welcome sensation that she immediately came.

Through the haze of her climax she felt Flare bend his head and take her swollen clit between his lips. His finger began to thrust in and out of her quaking flesh, impaling her over and over again. The muscles of her cunt squeezed his finger with each thrust, sending starbursts of pleasure exploding throughout her body.

She nearly passed out. Her vision did gray a bit around the edges, but she rallied her strength and her hands hugged his head tighter against her clit. Her body moved of its own volition, undulating wildly beneath his hands and mouth, pressing her pussy ever closer to his face. Her body was alive with sensations she never even dreamed of.

Flare's super-heated lips wandered up her body until he was kissing her mouth deeply once more. She could taste a trace of herself on his tongue but it didn't repulse her, it only made her hungrier for more and she kissed him back with a vengeance that surprised them both.

A moan escaped her lips as Flare pulled back and she reached to bring him back, but he caught her hands, kissed her palms and set them away from him.

"I'll be back in one second," he said, and just like that he vanished from the room.

She sat up and her yell of pure frustration made her feel better about his leaving, but before she could even think about moving farther, Flare appeared once more, still gloriously nude. All that golden bronze skin just made her mouth water! There was a fistful of condoms in his hand and Isis frowned. He bent his head to hers, his hot breath mingling with hers.

"I don't have any diseases," she said.

"Neither do I," he said with a quick, hard kiss to her lips. "But I need to protect you all the same."

"But I want to feel you naked inside me," she gasped out between kisses.

"Not yet," he said firmly.

He leaned back away from her and tossed all the condoms save one on her bedside table. Isis watched as his fingers quickly tore open the silver packet and placed the tip of the condom against the glistening tip of his cock. He rolled the condom up over him, stretching the material tight with his massive girth and length.

As soon as he was done Isis reached out and grabbed him, turning them so that he fell to the bed and she crawled up over his body, straddling him. For the very first time she was looking forward to what was coming next and it was a heady feeling. She'd never felt so free, so powerful as she did when she let her body sink down onto Flare's cock.

The feeling of fullness, of tightness, was almost painful, but Flare put his hands on her breasts and squeezed her nipples and she relaxed against him, sinking down farther. The tip of him was finally inside of her, but there was a long way yet to go and she wriggled her hips to eagerly force more of him inside of her.

Flare's hands immediately went to her hips and held her still. Then he slowly, gently lowered her over him.

He stretched her so tight that she cried out with the pleasure-pain, and her body clamped down on his.

One of his hands drifted down between her legs and found her clit. The rough pads of his fingers squeezed and rubbed the hard nubbin of flesh and her head fell back with renewed ecstasy. Her body relaxed once more and she sank down farther over him.

"Just a little bit more, baby." His words were low like a growl, yet soft and undemanding. "A little more, yeah, that's it," he praised as she kept sliding down around his dick. "Come on, baby. Take all of me."

Isis sank down the last few inches quickly and they both cried out their pleasure. He was so huge that he stole her breath away and boggled her mind. They stilled for several moments and then Flare began to guide her with his hands on her hips. He lifted her with a strength that stunned her, not straining in the least, and then he lowered her swiftly once more so that she caught her shriek of surprised pleasure in the back of her throat before it could escape.

Instinct took over and she began to ride him, not waiting for him to do the work by lifting her himself. Each stroke made them gasp and as her pace increased, so did the rhythm of their breathing.

The room was boiling hot now, as was Flare's skin. His cock, buried so deep and tight in her, was so hot it nearly scorched her tender flesh. But he kept himself just cool enough to titillate her with the threat of burning her up completely. He didn't need his fire to do that anyway. Only his kiss, his touch, his voice—these were enough to keep her hot and wet and ready.

Her breasts bounced as she slid up and down on him. He brought both hands back to her breasts, fingers gently rolling her nipples, and held them still for her.

So quickly that it astonished them both, Isis came again. Her body clamped down on his, so tight that Flare roared, and her pussy began to milk him with violent tremors. Flare thrust up high into her, lifting her body with his hips, and he shouted as he too joined her in climax.

Flare had never felt anything like this before. His cock was squeezed so tightly by her body that he could barely keep from ravaging her in his ever-mounting pleasure. He spurted into the condom so hard that he knew she had to feel the fire of his release through the rubber. His hands tightened on her breasts uncontrollably, but that only seemed to spur Isis onward in her trip to the heavens. His heartbeat was thick in his dick and he could feel Isis' pulse beat around him too.

Isis collapsed against him. He moaned long and low one last time as he shot the rest of his cum into the condom then gathered her close. He pressed a kiss to the sweat at her temple and put both his arms around her, soothing them both with long strokes from the back of her neck to the rise of her bottom.

The room cooled as their breathing slowed. Isis laid her head on Flare's chest and listened to his thundering heartbeat beneath her ear.

"You were magnificent," he whispered against the top of her hair.

The words made her feel like a goddess, and they were said so honestly, so openly that she knew it was true. She laughed with true happiness and teasingly bit his nipple. He swatted her behind, but only enough to make it sting sensually, and then he held her close again. He held her that way all through the night and Isis slept so deeply that she didn't feel it when he rose and left her, gently covering her with a blanket and disappearing into the glow of the coming dawn.

Chapter Seven

ഇ

Isis woke up alone, but she knew that Flare had had to go—none of her drapes were thick enough to block out the rays of the sun. She rose groggily, gasping when her body reminded her of her strenuous activity of the night before. Her body felt bruised and sore, but the soft pain was so delectable that she relished every ache and pain as she moved about.

She donned a robe and wandered through the house, heading for the kitchen. She rubbed her eyes blearily and gave a huge, satisfying yawn. It was amazing how good she felt and she was determined to hold onto that happy, contented feeling.

But fate was cruel. And as soon as she entered her kitchen she saw her sister's note laid out on the table as well as the fallen bottle of Jager. Painfully reminded that not all was going well in her life, Isis avoided looking at it as she went about making a bowl of cereal. However, the dangerous lure of the letter beat at her resolve and she sat at the table with a slump, her cereal growing soggy as she stared down at the words written on the paper.

It took Isis a long while to figure it out, but she realized with some surprise that she wasn't hurting as badly as she had when reading the note previously. The heavy, wrenching pain in her heart was barely there. Instead she found that she was angry.

Very angry.

"Damn you. Damn you *both*," she growled and slammed her fists down on the table, splintering the wood slightly on one side, surprising herself with the strength behind her blow.

Isis held her hands up before her face. They were shaking. "What's happening to me?" she asked in a soft whisper.

Silent and musing, Isis sat there, staring off into space for several long minutes. Coming to a decision, she rose and dressed and began to pack her meager belongings. All the furniture and appliances had come with the rental of the house. All she had were a few trinkets and some clothes and shoes. Still, it took her all morning and part of the afternoon to gather her things.

With her bags packed and the damned letter with its torn envelope in her front pocket, she sat down in the old, worn recliner in her sitting room and waited for Flare to arrive. She wasn't leaving without him. Even though she felt sure he could find her no matter where she went, she still wanted to wait for him and let him know that she was leaving.

With her savings she would have enough money to take her time shopping for a new rental. In the meantime she fully intended to stay at an old hotel she knew of that was over an hour away from her present location. She wanted nothing more than to get as much distance as possible between dwellings before the night ended.

The sun didn't set soon enough for her. But eventually, at last, there was no light in the room, and Flare appeared before her almost as soon as the sun disappeared over the horizon. Isis immediately went into his waiting arms and hugged him tight.

"I missed you this morning," she said, feeling a tad shy.

Flare smiled, revealing his lovely teeth. "I missed you all day." He motioned to her bags. "This is good. I was going to suggest you move now that the Daemons know where you live."

Isis hadn't even thought about that. "Yeah," she said slowly. "I was getting tired of this place anyway."

"Is this all you are taking?" he asked with a frown.

"It's all I have," she admitted.

"Are you ready to leave now?"

Isis smiled, relieved at Flare's expediency. "*Yes.* Can you help me—"

She didn't even get to finish because Flare had gathered all her bags and was already carrying them to the door. She followed him outside, locking up behind her and leaving the keys in an envelope taped to the door. Isis joined Flare at her car as he was putting the last bag into the trunk.

"I thought about heading to this hotel I know of. It's kind of far though," she explained.

"The farther we get from here the better, to my way of thinking," he answered, fitting his long legs into the front passenger's seat. Isis didn't know why she hadn't yet noticed just how huge he seemed in the car, but she definitely noticed now. She grinned, watching him squeeze into the car.

He looked up at her and caught her smile. "What?" he asked.

"You just look so funny," she admitted.

"Yes, well, Shikars are not built for human transportation. We much prefer Traveling."

Isis started the car and backed down the driveway. "Traveling? Is that what you call it when you disappear and reappear all the time?"

"Yes," he answered.

"I don't like it. All that whooshing air and confusion and that feeling like you're cut adrift from the real world is just too much for me. It makes my stomach ache just thinking about it."

"It can be unsettling at first," he nodded.

"One question though." She pulled onto the highway. "I saw that the Daemons Travel too. Why don't they just appear here in the car and kill us both right now?"

"That is a good question and one we have puzzled over in the recent years since Daemons have developed the ability to Travel. We think they're just clumsy, unable to focus on any one specific place and appear at will. Traveling is very draining—even to us Shikars. And the Daemons' destinations always seem random and accidental. You noticed that only one Daemon met you in your house—the others appeared outside of it."

"What does that mean though?" she asked.

"That the Daemon you faced was simply stronger than the other three in its pod," he told her flatly then sighed heavily. "I will never be able to forgive myself for letting that Daemon get to you," he admitted softly. "I am so sorry, Isis."

Isis snorted. "Don't be like that. It wasn't your fault at all. We both know that if you hadn't been there I would have been dead meat. I killed one measly Daemon — you killed three, remember?"

"Still, he hurt you. And I was not there to protect you."

"But you *were* there. And you made all my injuries go away." She glanced at him out of the corner of her eye. "Why do you think I did what I did to that monster?" she blurted.

Flare stared ahead at the road before them. "I told you that you were strong."

"Yeah, but strong like *that*? I tore that thing apart with my bare hands! God," she sighed. "I was so angry. I haven't been angry like that since — " She broke off abruptly, shocked at what she had so easily begun to say.

"Since when?" he prodded her mercilessly.

"It was a long time ago," she explained and hoped he'd leave it at that.

He didn't. "Tell me anyway." He made the words a command.

Isis thought in silence for several minutes. "I can't tell you," she admitted finally. "It's too hard right now." She put her hand out and caught his, entwining their fingers together and squeezing it tight. "But I promise I *will* tell you someday. Just give me a little more time, okay?"

Flare looked like he wanted to press her but she shook her head with gritted teeth, warning him away from the subject. He finally settled back in his seat, letting it go, and she breathed an audible sigh of relief. But Isis knew he would ask her about it again. Soon.

Isis wanted to fill the sudden silence. Her fraying nerves needed small talk to distract her from her stresses. "Tell me about your childhood," she said, knowing it was hypocritical of her to expect him to tell her anything when she wouldn't tell him the one thing he seemed to want to know the most, but it was all she could think to ask. Besides, she *was* interested in his past—very. Isis wanted to know all about who he was.

Flare seemed inclined to humor her. "My parents were both very loving. My father and mother are gone but the rest of our family is very close, even now after all the years. When I was born it wasn't clear what Caste of warrior I would be, so my parents waited to name me until I showed my first Shikar traits."

"So kids are the same with Shikars as they are with humans?"

"Very much so. Our kind is not so different as you might think. We have the same needs as humans—food, shelter, water—the basics."

"I've never seen you eat," she remarked.

"Shikars do not need to eat as much as humans do. We eat every couple of days or so. Our metabolic rate is very different from yours."

"Neat," she said with a grin, feeling some of her cares being soothed away by the magic in Flare's voice. "So when did you first exhibit your Shikar powers?"

"When I was three. I don't remember it, but apparently I set my bedroom on fire."

Isis gasped. "Are you serious? Oh my God, your parents must have been scared shitless."

Flare laughed. "No. My father put the flames out easily enough and my mother immediately had my bedroom redesigned in stone so that such a thing couldn't happen again. Not that the fire would have hurt me, but it could have hurt other Shikars and it was just safer to avoid using wood in my environment."

"That's why your whole apartment is done in stone. I just thought it was to be ostentatious."

"It is safest that way. I haven't lost control of my power in a long time — usually it happens during one's sleep, but I'm a light sleeper by nature so I usually check myself before anything destructive happens. But sometimes there are unavoidable accidents and the stonework is simply a precaution against that."

"Sounds reasonable," she said with a nod.

"My aunt and uncle live a few miles from me but—"

"Holy hell, are you telling me that your underground city is that big?"

Flare threw a long lock of hair back behind his shoulder. "I think the city is about as big as your New York City. Maybe bigger."

"Oh my God, are you serious?" Isis was truly incredulous. As big as New York City. Shit.

"I'm not sure. It grows daily — whenever a warrior mates he leaves the bachelor quarters and moves into new quarters designed specifically to meet the couple's needs. And when male children become warriors, they are given their own home — a haven away from our constant battles with the Daemons. Usually new apartments are dug out of the rock specifically for each new warrior who reaches maturity—though not always. Sometimes there's a vacancy due to one of the warriors mating. My apartment, though, was specially constructed to my specifications."

"What about the women?" Isis had noticed he'd said male children become warriors and said nothing about the females. "Are they part of your army?"

"Hmm," Flare mused thoughtfully. "None of our females have ever wanted to be warriors—not that I know of. In our culture the females usually stay behind to protect the children and to make a home for the family. In return, their mates provide safety, love and constant protection. But there are four females—humans like yourself—who have joined the ranks of warriors and fight alongside the males."

Isis was interested in this. "Do you know these women personally?"

"I know *of* them. Everyone does—they're already legendary among us. Their names are Cady, Steffy, Emily and Nikki. They're all different yet strong and valiant beyond any humans we have ever known." He deliberately neglected to tell her that the women had long since become Shikars themselves, thanks to their mates.

"Do you have any other family?"

"Many aunts and uncles. No brothers or sisters though—my parents had enough on their hands with me as their son." He chuckled. "I was a bit of a hellion in my youth. Stubborn as an ox and cocky too. I've mellowed a lot since then though."

Isis could almost imagine him as a boy—precocious, prone to getting into mischief, proud of his powers and adventurous to a fault.

The dark figure in the middle of the road appeared out of nowhere and there was nothing Isis could do to keep from hitting it. She shrieked in surprise and jerked the wheel but she was far too slow in her reaction. Her car slammed into the figure as if it were a giant slab of concrete, crumpling the front end of her vehicle. The figure bounced off the hood, shattered her windshield and landed limply in the road behind them. The car skidded and went into a spin as she slammed on the brakes in alarm. The spin ended with them facing away from whatever it was that they'd hit. Isis' car stalled and suddenly everything went quiet but for Isis' panicked breaths.

"Oh my sweet holy God! That was a man! I hit him, oh fuck, oh fuck, oh fuck!" Isis knew she was babbling but she couldn't stop it. Adrenaline surged through her and she struggled with the door handle—her hands were shaking so bad it made her clumsy and she fumbled a few times before Flare put his hand on her shoulder and pulled her away from the door.

"Are you hurt?" he asked her, hands already feeling her for injuries.

"I'm fine," she answered with a gasp—even now his touch ignited heat within her.

"Get the car started again," he told her. "I'll go take care of our friend."

"Is it a Daemon?" she asked, words coming so fast she was surprised he could understand her.

"Yes. And I think there might be more nearby," he told her, exiting the car. "Stay put," he commanded as he closed his door.

Isis felt immediate, sweet relief wash over her. "Thank God," she said then anger replaced her panic. "That motherfucker just destroyed my car," she yelled in agitation. She tried the ignition—the car sputtered a few times but the engine wouldn't turn over. She tried again. And again. She decided to let the car sit for a few moments to see if that might help.

A bright explosion of light behind her drew her attention and she turned around in her seat to watch Flare set the battered body of the Daemon aflame. Out of the corner of her eye she saw a dark form running unbelievably fast toward Flare.

Not caring about her own safety, she opened her car door and got out as fast as she could manage. "Flare, look out," she screamed. But she needn't have done so— Flare had already turned and he immediately set the racing Daemon aflame. The beast screamed and continued to run toward Flare, intent only on its evil purpose. They met in the middle of the road and Flare instantly plunged his hands into the burning monster's rib cage, wrenching the heart out with one efficient tug. The monster fell and shuddered. When Flare set the heart in his hand aflame, the monster abruptly lay still as if a switch had turned it off.

Isis approached Flare, careful to skirt around the pile of ash in the middle of the road. "Is it dead?" she asked, watching it burn.

Flare turned to her and his eyes were alight with anger. "I told you to stay in the car," he said in a stony voice. Isis was shocked—but then she should have expected it from him. He took his mission of protecting her very seriously. She supposed his iron will was what made him such a formidable warrior.

Two more Daemons appeared, roaring and charging at Flare an instant after they arrived. Isis scrambled backward then ran back to the car as the battle made its way toward her. She jumped—thinking to crawl up on the trunk of the vehicle and climb her way over the top to scramble into her car.

But her jump took her much farther. With just the power of her legs she managed to launch herself several feet into the air. She came down, hard, onto the asphalt in front of her car, but she landed on her feet. Isis was in a state of shock. She had cleared the *entire* vehicle with just one jump.

Isis quickly recovered and ran to her car door. She climbed into the mangled vehicle and tried to crank it. Three tries later the engine sputtered once, twice, then turned over and the car roared to life as she gave it some gas to help it along.

The glow behind her intensified, lighting up the night sky. Isis knew he had disposed of the last two Daemons as quickly as he had the first two. Seconds later Flare opened the passenger door and got into the car once more.

"Are you okay?" she asked, worried.

"I am not happy with you," he growled low. "Drive."

"*What*? I was trying to save your hide, you ungrateful brute," she yelled back, automatically putting the car in drive and pulling away from the battle scene.

"Besides," she lowered her voice, "I'm not one of your soldiers. You can't expect me to do everything you tell me to."

"I can and I do expect just that. Any orders I give you are given for good reason. You put yourself in danger by getting out of the car and coming out into the open." He gritted his teeth audibly, as if he was fighting the urge to shout. "You are never to endanger yourself like that again. Not even for me. *Especially* not for me."

"But I lo—" Isis broke off with a shocked choke of air. She couldn't believe what she had almost just said to him.

Had he noticed her slip? God she hoped not.

Did she love him already? No. It was way too soon for that, she told herself, ignoring the pang in her heart that came with the thought. She tried to cover up her near admission of something she'd never admitted to *anyone* but her mother with her next words. "I care about you, Flare," she said. "I don't want you to get hurt because of me."

"It is my sacred duty to protect you," he said somberly. "What happens to me is my concern, not yours. Your only concern is to keep yourself as far away from the Daemons as possible. As far out of harm's reach as you can manage."

"You can't tell me what to do," she said mutinously.

"I can and I will. You *will* obey me, Isis. I will have it no other way," he said arrogantly. The temperature within the confines of the car rose several degrees.

It was true that he had been displeased to see her get out of the car when he'd told her to stay put. But what Flare didn't tell her was that his heart had nearly given out when he'd seen her jump over the car. She'd done it so effortlessly, so gracefully — never had he witnessed anything like it. He'd been more afraid that she'd land roughly and hurt herself than he had been about the Daemons he was fighting. He'd been amazed when she'd landed flat on her feet. But the lingering fear she'd inspired in him had not yet waned.

He knew that he was being a brute. But Isis was so hardheaded — she needed a strong arm to guide her through this dangerous time. She didn't need his tenderness so much now — she needed his discipline and, yes, even his ire. It was the only way he knew how to get through to her, how best to protect her.

Studying her reaction to his words, he noted how tightly she gripped the steering wheel — her knuckles were bone white. He could hear the grinding of her teeth and her deliciously full lips were pursed tightly. Yet she held her silence, though he sensed she wanted to scream and rail at him. Isis wasn't happy with him right now, but Flare was sure she'd be more careful in the future.

Isis too was giving thought to her amazing feat of jumping the length of her car. A bit of a plan was beginning to form in her mind — it was still rough around the edges, but she was sure, once Flare got used to it, that things would work out in the end. The real question was how to broach the subject with him.

She wanted to be a warrior. Just like those other human women he'd told her about. It was scary — the thought of fighting the monsters on a regular basis — but it was also tantalizing to know she'd be keeping humankind safe from a great evil. Isis liked that idea very much.

It was likely that Flare would have a conniption fit once she told him of her intent, but she was stubborn enough to know that eventually she could wear him down if she tried hard enough. He took protecting her very seriously—that was more than obvious now—but she knew he was also very mindful of wanting to please her and keep her happy. Once he saw how much she wanted this, perhaps he would relent and let her do it.

Isis knew she was physically strong enough to do it. She'd exhibited that more than once in the last couple days. But was she mentally capable of handling such a responsibility after so many years of being alone and apathetic? That was the real quandary. She just didn't know.

The rest of the drive was silent and it was a test of her will not to say anything to Flare about her idea, but she knew he was having a hard time getting control of himself so soon after the battle. He seemed to need the silence and she let him have it. Besides, she was more than used to being quiet. Well, most of the time.

Chapter Eight

ɞ

When the crippled car rattled into the parking space outside their hotel room, Flare retrieved her bags from the car before she could even think to. He entered the room first and checked every corner to ensure there was no threat. Isis had to admire his thoroughness. He was determined to honor his duty.

"I do not like this place," he told her at last. "It is too open for attack and your car parked just outside is an obvious giveaway to our location. Look—the door is even weak." He went over and jiggled the handle of the flimsy wooden door at the entrance. "I could easily break in, and if I can, then so could a Daemon."

"Well, it's the best I could do on short notice," she told him with a huff.

"I want you to stay at a better lit hotel. One where the rooms are on the inside. One where there are more people—staying in a public place might keep you safer from the threat hanging over your head."

"I've already paid in full for the night," she explained.

"It does not matter. I have plenty of money. Let's leave," he urged.

Isis shook her head. "I don't need your money. Look, let's just stay here for tonight and I'll find a better hotel tomorrow, okay? Promise."

The room heated up and it was more than apparent that Flare wanted to argue with her further. He started to, but Isis gave him her back and went into the bathroom, closing the door behind her with a soft click of the lock as she pushed in the tiny knob on the door handle.

It didn't matter. Flare pushed the door open easily, breaking the frame and splintering the wood. "Do *not* walk away from me when I am talking to you," he growled. Heat baked off him in strong waves.

"I thought we were finished," she said lightly, putting her hair up in a ponytail with the use of the mirror above the bathroom sink. God but it was hot in here!

"You knew we were not finished," he said pointedly, gaze smoldering.

"Look, Flare, I don't want to argue anymore. I'm staying here tonight. If the Daemons find us we'll leave. But for now this is as good a place as any—I don't even know where a decent hotel is around here anyway."

Flare glared at her. "You won't listen to reason. Perhaps you will listen to this." He jerked her to him and pressed a hard kiss to her mouth. Then he lifted her off her feet and carted her back out of the bathroom. He tossed her roughly on the bed and the springs groaned their protest so loudly that for a moment Isis feared the bed would collapse.

What she expected next from Flare did not happen. There were no more kisses. No more caresses. Instead, Flare flipped her onto her stomach and yanked her jeans down around her ankles without any difficulty. Isis wasn't stupid—she now knew what Flare intended.

The sound of the first slap on her bottom was drowned out by her scream of pure rage. She struggled beneath him, bucking wildly and kicking out with her legs. Flare spanked her again, making her ass cheeks grow hot.

It wasn't that he hit her hard. He didn't—though his hand was scorching hot when it connected with her sensitive skin. It was that he would humiliate her so that enraged her.

With another roar she managed to kick him hard in the shin, forcing him back a little. Bucking wildly, she took the opportunity and rolled away from him, kicking off her jeans to free up her legs. She was now nude from the waist down but she didn't even care. Before he could stop her, she jumped off the bed and came at him, punching him squarely in the cheek. Isis knew her blow had to hurt—the imprint of her knuckles was already stained on his cheek and her hand stung fiercely. But Flare never flinched. Nor did he do what she feared he might do—force her back into submission.

They stood there, face-to-face like longtime enemies, breathing heavily.

"Don't ever do that," Isis told him in her hardest tone, anger making her shake uncontrollably. "I mean it."

"I just want you to know how important it is that you let me take care of you. If the Daemons were to get you, our entire race would be in danger, as well as yours. Not to mention that it would kill me if you were hurt or captured," he explained passionately. "But you can be so stubborn and thickheaded—it makes me so frustrated!

You refuse to listen to reason. I don't know how else to reach you."

"Spanking me will only result in you getting hurt," she told him from behind clenched teeth. "So. You don't want to stay here tonight? Fine. Get out." Isis pointed toward the door, looking away.

Suddenly she was in his arms again, and the passion with which he kissed her made her toes curl despite her anger. He lifted her again, more gently this time, and laid her back down on the bed, coming down over her. "I am sorry," he told her, dotting her face with kisses, turning the heat of her anger into another kind of heat entirely. She could see that he meant the apology, even if her senses were swamped by being held half naked beneath him. "But I must stay in control of this situation. Surely you understand that, Isis?"

Isis wouldn't meet his eyes. "I've had far worse things done to me than this. I forgive you. Just don't ever do it again—I hate it. It makes me feel helpless. Powerless. All sorts of bad things. I won't forgive you again." She wasn't sure if that was true or not. She was used to being beaten—she had been dealt with violently her whole childhood in one way or another, but she didn't want to associate Flare with that kind of violence. Not in any way.

"I just want to keep you safe," he murmured, kissing her forehead gently.

"You *are* keeping me safe." she said. "I don't have any fears or worries when you're near me and that is more wonderful than you'll ever know." It was hard for her to admit that, even to herself, but it was the truth. "I know you won't let anything happen to me. But I need to rest. I've had a really hard day. I don't want to drive anymore tonight, wandering through the boonies, looking for another place to stay."

"All right," he told her. "But tomorrow you'll find a safer place to stay."

"I will," she promised, more than agreeable. "Now kiss me some more, you brute." She smiled shyly up at him.

Flare didn't need to be told twice. He covered her mouth with his own, his tongue seeking out and finding hers immediately. It stunned her how fast the anger was replaced by passion. Isis kissed him back hungrily, her fingers tangling in the silky soft hair that fell down his back.

It was amazing how quickly she'd become addicted to his touch. His hands roved all over her, lingering on her naked skin then moving to pull off her shirt. Her bra was clasped in the back, making it difficult for Flare to remove it. He growled after a few tries and then moved his hand back around to her front. A tiny blade-looking thing shot out of his fingertip. It was glowing red-hot. And when he traced his finger over the delicate material of her bra—careful not to touch her skin—it fell away, freeing her breasts to his gaze and touch.

"Hold your breasts for me," he said, squeezing one erect nipple gently. "Hold them and play with your nipples," he urged.

Isis knew how important visual stimulation was for men to become aroused. "I'll do you one better," she told him. She pushed him away and rose from the bed. "Watch this," Isis said with a wicked smile, and she began to dance.

Already naked, there was no need to strip, and dancing completely nude was easier than hiding everything between her legs behind the panties she was required to wear onstage. Amazingly, for the first time ever, she was growing aroused by her own dancing. And the burning heat in Flare's eyes only spurred her on, melting her insides.

Undulating, she turned and gave him her back. She stood with her feet apart and bent over, grabbing one of her ankles with both of her hands. She heard Flare's moan as she showed him all of her secrets and smiled to herself. Slowly, sensually, she ran her hands up her leg and resumed dancing.

When she turned to face him again she clearly saw that Flare was close to losing some of that iron control he always had over himself. He looked as if he was about to jump her.

Isis laughed happily and continued to dance. She undulated her hips, running her hands all over her body, pausing to finger her pussy and pinch her nipples to aching hardness. When she did this, Flare's gaze could have burnt a hole in the wall. And the temperature of the room was rising rapidly. Isis glanced down and saw that he had actually singed fingerprints into the bedclothes as he clutched the edge of the bed, holding tight as if to keep from launching himself at her and ravaging her completely. With a practiced move she released her hair and whipped it about her head as she moved and waited for his reaction.

It was swift and immediate. Before she could blink twice, Flare had her up against the wall. He freed his cock from his pants, lifted her up and thrust into her with one fierce shove of his hips. She was so wet from her own arousal that, though it was a tight fit, he slid in easily enough and they both moaned. He made her put her legs around his waist so that his hands could freely wander over her whole body. His touch was so hot she knew there would be marks on her in the morning where his fingertips lingered.

But she didn't care. It felt *so* good.

And the heat of his cock inside her stole her breath away. He was burning up! Sweat had already popped up on her brow and across the bridge of her nose. She panted for air that wasn't stiflingly hot, but Flare caught her mouth and gave her his sultry breath instead, filling her with the taste and feel of him so not even a tiny bit of her being wasn't laid claim to in some manner.

The entire length of her body was laid to waste as he touched every inch of her flesh, stroking her from head to toe. Her head kept bumping against the wall every time he thrust into her—entering her with such force that it should have bruised her. Yet it didn't.

"Oh, Isis, I need you so much," he gasped, lips pressing to the curve of her neck and shoulder. He suckled her skin between his teeth, leaving behind a red mark that wouldn't fade for days.

Isis clutched at him, her hands holding on to the bulging muscles of his upper arms. Her fingernails dug into his skin every time he bounced her back against the wall. His cock drove into her until she was keening high in the back of her throat uncontrollably, her pleasure so extreme it made tears leak out of the corners of her eyes.

Her climax hit her hard and intense. Her body clamped down on his, her pussy milking his cock with her tremors. He stayed with her, keeping Isis at the pinnacle of passion for as long as he could.

The climax was so strong it sapped her of all strength. Her body, abuzz with a heart-wrenching emotion she couldn't name, shuddered around his. Her head fell weakly against his chest, her breath bellowing out of her lungs.

Flare pulled his body free from hers and carried her to the bed. He reached into a tiny black silk bag secured at his waist and pulled out a condom. Ripping the packet open with his teeth, he hurriedly sheathed his cock in its protective covering with trembling fingers and came down to cover her body with his hot one.

Just knowing that she affected him so much that his control was slipping before the force of their passion made her need for him rise once again. If Flare didn't hurry, she would be begging him to take her again.

Then he was inside of her once more, stretching and filling her to bursting, and she screamed out her pleasure. Flare's fingers moved between them and found her clit. He pinched it, rubbed it, using her moisture to make his fingertips more slippery against her, bombarding her with endless pleasure, stimulating her so that she flew to the precipice of another climax in a matter of minutes.

Flare caught both her ankles and put them around his neck, tilting her hips up so that he penetrated her even more deeply. His hips pistoned over and over between her legs and she arched closer to receive his forceful thrusts, riding him with sensual undulations of her hips. His rhythm increased and the bed groaned its protest. Neither cared, they clutched at each other, their hands roving all over their naked skin, lingering in all the right places, still pounding away at each other.

Groaning, Flare found her clit once more. "Come for me again, baby," he commanded, pushing her to the edge with little effort. "Come on," he groaned, long and loud.

Isis clutched him tight and screamed as she came, the sensations of pure pleasure bombarding her so that she was mindless to anything else. She barely heard Flare's own shout of release, but there was no mistaking the hot feel of his cum spurting inside of her, into the tip of the condom.

Boneless and sapped of all strength, Isis collapsed into the bed. Flare followed her, turning so that his body did not crush her, but the bed instead. The poor, abused thing gave one final groan and the bed frame broke, dropping them straight onto the hard floor with a thud.

"I am so not paying for that," she said breathlessly then laughed. "We've, like, totally demolished this place already, you know that."

"And we have the whole night to finish off the job." He grinned at her, tucking an errant lock of hair behind her ear. "By Grimm, but you are so pretty, Isis."

His words brought out a blush in her cheeks—something she didn't even think she was capable of—even though she had no idea who or what Grimm was. "I think you're beautiful," she told him softly, shyly, turning on her side to better see him as he reclined beside her.

Flare frowned and his eyes seemed to glow from within. "Get up, Isis," he told her.

"What's happening?"

"Just get up. Take my hand." He took hers in his before she could comply.

"Wait a minute," she cried and pulled away from him so abruptly that he had no choice but to let her go or risk injuring her. Running to where she had flung her jeans, Isis delved into its pockets and found the envelope containing her sister's letter. "Okay, I'm ready," she said hurriedly, rushing back to him, unconcerned with her nudity.

"Hold on to me," he said, clutching her tight to his smoldering body.

The whole world melted away and she closed her eyes tightly shut as they Traveled out of the way of danger.

* * * * *

Moments later her vision cleared and she saw that they were standing in Flare's enormous sitting room. Isis was shivering in reaction to the strange sensation of Traveling. Flare, thinking she was cold, pulled her close and raised his body temperature enough to banish any chill. "It's all right now. We are safe here," he said in an effort to further soothe her.

"I want some clothes," she said at once.

Flare let her go slowly, as if he didn't want to. He went into his bedroom and opened a great armoire that looked as if it had been made completely of soapstone. Isis stood framed in the door as he rummaged through some clothing within, and came back to her with another dated-looking, royal purple baby doll dress for her to wear, plus some black clothing for himself.

"I've been meaning to ask you—why do you have women's clothing in your room?" She looked at him in a playfully suspicious manner.

Flare, realizing that she was going to be all right, sighed his relief and grinned as he dressed. "I had some of the females here donate their clothes for just such an occasion. I knew eventually you'd come here, so I got a few things to fit you. Just in case."

Isis snorted. "You planned to get me naked all along, didn't you?"

Flare laughed and the sound of it made her heart race. "I had hoped."

"Why you sneaky devil." She snorted again and put on the dress. "I don't suppose you've got any underwear in there?"

Flare's eyes widened. "I forgot," he said, surprised. He went back into the room and this time Isis followed him. He rummaged through the armoire again, taking much longer this time, before he came up with a handful of red satin. "We have seamstresses who do nothing but design lingerie for our mated women. Here, these should fit." He handed the scraps of cloth to her.

There was a very cute red bra made of what *looked* like satin, but the cloth felt far too soft. The crimson panties were the same, cut high on the leg with a darker red triangle over her pussy. This feature, Isis knew instinctively, was to draw the eye straight to her sex. "Naughty," she said with a chuckle as she put the lingerie on beneath her dress.

"Do you want anything to eat or drink?" he asked her.

"I *am* thirsty," she admitted.

Flare approached the fireplace that was placed along one wall of his sitting room. He knelt down and lit a fire by laying his hand on the wooden logs that were already stacked there. The logs flared brightly hot in less than a few seconds and a roaring fire sprang into light.

With a self-satisfied nod, Flare rose to his feet once more. He opened a jewel-encrusted box on the mantle and took out a handful of what looked to Isis like colorful sand.

"This," Flare turned to show her, "is fl'shan powder. We use it for many things. I mostly use it for this." He threw it into the fire and the flame flared dangerously high for a second before settling down again. "I need two cups of tea," he said, aiming his words at the fireplace.

He turned and noticed her frown of confusion. "We can talk through the fire with the powder. I just asked one of the kitchen workers to bring our drinks."

"Kitchen workers? You don't have to make your own food?"

"No. I am a warrior. My needs are seen to with little effort. I've been thankful for that my whole life—especially after battles. When I'm wounded or tired I just call for what I need and it is almost instantly brought to me."

"So the kitchen workers are like your servants?"

"No," he said in a shocked tone. "They're volunteers. Mostly unmated women who have no one to cook for. No one here is a servant," he said with great pride. "We men grow to be warriors. Some of us eventually go into the politics of keeping our way of life running smoothly, but we all have some kind of battle experience. The women grow to be equally as strong, but they are gentle by nature and more nurturing. They all have jobs to do, but they only take on the tasks they wish. Things that they enjoy."

"You have politics here?"

"We have a Council of Elders. Older warriors who have earned the rank through hard work and self-sacrifice."

"How old do you have to be to be an Elder?" she asked curiously.

"Usually at least three hundred years old."

Isis felt her eyes bulge. "Three hundred? Jesus fucking Christ! How long do you people live?"

"We live as long as we are meant to."

"How old are you?" She frowned suspiciously.

"I am two hundred and seven years old," he said.

Isis gasped. "No fucking way. You look like you're in your early thirties."

"Shikars do not age like humans. We do not grow to old age as your kind does. We stop aging at about thirty, sometimes forty."

"Oh my God."

"Does my age make you feel any differently about me?"

Isis saw the worry in his eyes that she would say yes. She thought about it and found that, no, it didn't matter to her. But it was definitely weird. "No. But I must seem like a real adolescent to you."

"Not in any way," he assured her.

There came the sound of a bell ringing. Isis glanced at the entrance and saw a small brass bell above the door, connected to a string that led out of the door to the other side. Isis supposed such a thing was quite useful. It would be hard for someone to hear a knock on a solid stone door, no matter how keen their hearing might be.

A tall, lithe woman with ankle-length blonde hair came into the room with a tray. She was the first Shikar besides Flare that Isis had ever seen. The woman was delicately beautiful, not at all brutish like her male counterpart. Yet she carried the heavy silver tray with an easy strength. Her skin was like cream, smooth and unblemished in any way, perfect. And her eyes were the same color as Flare's.

The woman gave Isis a curious glance but said nothing. She went into the sitting room with her tray and set it down on the stone coffee table.

"Hello, Sence," Flare said by way of welcome.

Sence smiled at him with a fondness that had Isis clenching her fists in jealousy. "I brought you some bread and cheese in case you were hungry," Sence said.

"Thank you," Flare said gently.

The woman gave Isis one last glance before she left the way she had come. Isis relaxed, her jealousy waning, cooling her rising ire. She shook the remnants away with a physical toss of her head.

Flare took a cup of steaming warm tea and offered her the other. "It's sweetened," he warned her.

She liked her tea sweet anyway. Isis took a sip of the brown liquid and raised her eyebrows at Flare. "This is delicious. This makes normal tea taste positively bitter."

"The leaves are grown in specially designed gardens. Our livestock is in a large grazing area, though our animals have evolved separately from their brethren on the surface world. They may seem odd to you, were you to see them. But I am assured that their meat tastes pretty much the same from either place."

Isis reached out and took a small square piece of cheese. She bit into it then smiled. It tasted just like Colby cheese, which she happened to like very much.

Flare finished his tea with one final gulp and set the cup down on the tray. He looked at her for a long while, as if he were trying to see into her very soul. He seemed to come to some decision and nodded to himself.

"I have to leave you here for a little while. I won't be far. I just need to meet with my superior about something," he told her. "It won't take long."

Isis understood. He was a soldier first and foremost. "I'll just stay here," she said obviously.

Flare laughed and turned, leaving her standing there watching his retreating back. Her eyes couldn't resist taking in all of him—holy hell but he had a sexy ass!

Flare reached the door and stepped through it, closing the entrance to his apartment behind him softly. Curious, Isis went and reached for the door handle. It turned easily in her hand. Flare hadn't locked her in. She smiled, satisfied, and went back into the sitting room to sit and daydream until her lover's return.

* * * * *

Flare knew he had given no notice, but The Generator, an Elder on the Council and his direct superior, welcomed him into his home as if he'd been expecting Flare's visit. The taller man motioned for him to enter and Flare stepped over the threshold, knowing that there would be no turning back from the course he was about to set for himself.

He only hoped he could get the approval of The Generator.

"How goes your mission?" the man asked as they settled into two great throne-like chairs, sitting opposite each other. The light in the room was soft, casting eerie shadows about them. The Elder had long black hair with tiny streaks of silver that looked as if they'd been artfully placed there and it reflected the light like a mirror. His eyes were a golden fire beneath artfully arched brows, just like all Shikars' eyes save those of the Traveler Caste, and he regarded Flare with those eyes now.

"That is what I have come to discuss with you."

"Things, I gather, have not gone as planned," The Generator said sagely.

Flare shook his head. "No they have not, Elder. My mission began easily enough but things have gotten...complicated." He had to force the word out.

The Generator smiled as if he knew just how complicated Flare's mission had become and why. "Your charge is safe, I take it? It is still dark in her part of the Territories. I can only assume you have her here with you, for I know you would not shirk your duty."

"No, Elder." Flare disguised his shock that The Generator already knew so much of what he'd come to tell him. "She is here. Now. And I come to you because of this."

"Continue," The Generator said patiently, steepling his long-fingered hands beneath his strong chin.

"I have come to ask your permission to allow Isis to stay with me. Permanently."

The Generator sat back in his seat, his golden eyes somber. "She is a human."

"I know," Flare nodded.

"You have lain with her?"

Flare squared his shoulders. "Yes."

The Generator nodded sagely and was silent for long moments. "This woman—"

"Isis," Flare said firmly.

The Generator's mouth curved in a shadow of a smile. "Isis, then. How strong is her attachment to you?"

"It is very strong," Flare said confidently. "Growing more so with each passing day."

The Generator regarded him for a moment. "You love her," he said, as if it was a discovery he had not expected. "Don't you?"

Flare thought hard. *Did* he love her? He searched his heart. He thought of life without her and the very idea was unacceptable to him. Flare had made his decision. "I do love her," he admitted. "I would make her my mate, if she would have me."

"But what if she won't? You know our rules. You cannot endanger a human woman—our seed is *poison* to them and quick to kill them."

"Not if they are strong. Not if they love their mate."

The Generator leaned forward, his hair falling so that it cast his face in a dark shadow. "But does this woman—Isis—love you?"

"She *will* love me," he said confidently.

"You must be sure before you try what we both know you will inevitably do."

Flare clenched his jaw. "Four women have become Shikar warriors. Isis is as strong, if not stronger, than they are. She has the power to fight against her death. Our love will carry her the rest of the way through and she will arise from her death as a Shikar. I am certain of it."

"It is beyond dangerous," The Generator said patiently.

Flare took a deep breath. "I know. But I am a strong Traveler—I can follow her into death and save her soul. The threat to her will be minimal. I will do all in my power to protect her."

"*If* she loves you," The Generator pressed ruthlessly. "It all hinges on love and the power of that great emotion, as well as her strength as a psychic. Remember this as you have never remembered anything else in your life. I forbid you to try changing her until you know for a certainty that her heart belongs to you. I will not have the unfortunate death of so strong a human on my conscience. Or yours."

"May she stay here in the meanwhile?" Flare asked respectfully.

The Generator sat back in his seat once more and Flare could see the look of concern clearly written on the Elder's face. "You may keep her here as long as the threat to her life in the Territories demands. But if you cannot convince her to tie her life to yours, you will return her to her world as soon as that threat is neutralized. Or as soon as she decides she must leave. If such a thing occurs you may not force her to stay." The

Generator's last words were laced with steel that demanded obedience.

"Yes, Elder." Flare nodded his assent, though he fully intended to keep Isis no matter the circumstances.

"In the interim you will return to your patrol duties in the Territories."

"Yes, Elder," Flare repeated with much respect.

"Now, go see to your woman. She must be wondering what you're up to. Humans are endlessly curious." The Generator dismissed him.

Glad to have the approval of his Elder, Flare left the room without looking back, eager to return to Isis with utmost haste.

Chapter Nine

ౠ

Isis jerked awake when Flare reentered the room. He'd been gone so long she'd grown bored and had apparently fallen asleep in the strange, alien quiet around her. She was used to at least the humming of the insects and frogs outside her window, and this silence was simply deafening.

"Is your business finished?" she asked, rising.

Flare smiled at her tenderly. "Yes. Everything has been arranged."

"What's been arranged?" Isis pressed.

"I have been given permission to offer you refuge here, with me, until the threat to you has been neutralized," he said, cautiously gauging her reaction to his softly spoken words.

There was no mistaking the spark of relief he saw in her eyes. She quickly schooled her face into a mask, hiding her reaction, but not before Flare could catch the telltale emotion. "That sounds good to me," she agreed.

"I have been instructed to resume my post as a patrol for the Territories, so I will be gone for at least six hours every night."

"Night and day don't seem to mean much here," she noted. "I mean, you can Travel anywhere in the world. You could go to France and I could sleep the day away, waiting for you to return when it would be night in my part of the world."

"This is true," Flare agreed. "I will arrange my schedule to fit yours so that we can spend your nights together."

Isis' gaze heated with sudden passion and Flare felt even surer of his intentions with this human woman. "It's still night in my part of the globe," she drawled with a sultry smile.

"You need your rest," he teased.

Isis huffed, blowing a lock of hair out of her face. "I just rested," she complained. "See." She put her arms out and turned in a circle. "Look at me. I'm totally not tired now."

"Promise?" he asked with a sly smile.

"I promise." Isis was already growing breathless with excitement.

"Well, I guess I'll have to be the judge of that," he said and stalked toward her. He caught her up in his arms and carried her from the sitting room to his bedroom. He gently placed her on his bed, fanning her hair out on his pillows so that he could admire its striking color against the silken sheets.

As gently as he knew how, he put his hands on the hem of her dress and began to push it up, stroking the skin that bared in its wake with the rough pads of his fingertips. "You're so soft," he murmured in wonder.

Reaching for him, Isis tugged at his shirt—she hadn't noticed before but it was made of some strange, almost rubber material, though it seemed to breathe well enough for he wasn't sweating. The materials used here in this world were surprising and strange. Isis tugged at the shirt until Flare took over and removed it, revealing all that lovely golden skin for her to admire at her leisure.

Flare pulled her dress up over her head and tossed it behind him negligently. She saw his eyes brighten when he caught sight of her lingerie and she devilishly wriggled free from it in the most seductive manner she knew how...and she knew a *lot* about stripping for a man's pleasure. Nude now, Isis rolled away from him playfully and he pounced on her with a mock growl, pressing her stomach into the thick cushion of the mattress. He kissed the back of her neck, brushing her hair so that it was over her shoulder. Isis gasped when he bit her there, but he quickly laved the tiny pain away with his hot tongue.

"I want to lay claim to your very soul," he whispered against her skin.

Isis was scared to death that he already had.

Flare inhaled her scent. "You smell fantastic," he told her, nuzzling her between her shoulder blades, using his lips and tongue to tickle and tease until she was panting excitedly.

Leaving not one inch of her skin unexplored by his mouth, he moved down her back and kissed the crown of her buttocks. Isis tried to turn over, but he held her still with one hand while the other traced the crevice of her bottom. Isis melted and any thought of shyness disappeared instantly. Flare released her and used both his hands to plump and squeeze her ass cheeks.

Wrenching a scream from her, he pressed his lips to the moue of her anus. Again Isis tried reflexively to get away. She rose to her knees, but that only opened her more fully for Flare's wicked exploration. He tongued her there, burning her tender flesh, and she cried out again in the face of the pleasure his caress demanded.

Her whole body clenched with need. The flicker of his tongue on her anus stole any coherent thought away from her and she was mindless to everything but the sensations flooding through her. The loss of her control should have frightened her, but she felt so safe and secure with Flare that not even a trace of fear marred her exquisite pleasure.

His tongue wandered down until it slipped into the moisture of her pussy. Isis stretched like a cat, raising her rear higher into the air to welcome the feel of his tongue as it thrust in and out of her body. Her head was buried now in the plush pillows on his bed, her hair tangling as she thrashed it back and forth, moaning uncontrollably each time his tongue filled her, reaching to the heart of her.

Flare fumbled with the fastenings of his trousers and his cock sprang free, hot and heavy and ready. He reached over to the table by the bed and opened a drawer. It was full of condoms — he'd been wise enough to know he would need a good supply of them. Grabbing one impatiently, all the while letting his other hand stroke Isis' silken body, he ripped the packet open with his teeth and rolled the condom over his sex.

Entering her from behind with one sure stroke, he leaned over her and held her breasts in his hands. His fingers plucked and squeezed at her diamond-hard nipples until she was panting and matching him thrust for thrust, and his hips cradled hers as he pumped his body into her repeatedly.

"Taste this bit of heaven for me now, baby," Flare commanded, his fingers stroking down her front, pausing only to tease and tickle her bellybutton before seeking out her clit. He began to rub little circles into the nubbin of flesh and Isis began to buck wildly beneath him, racing toward her climax.

It slammed into her with the force of a runaway freight train. She screamed, long and loud, the sound only barely muffled by the pillow she had instinctively bitten to silence her cry. Her head felt like it would explode into starbursts and her body felt as if it would melt into a puddle right there in the bed.

Flare joined her in passion's sweet reward, shouting his triumph to the heavens as he shot his cum deep into the heart of her. Despite the condom, Isis felt the scalding heat of his seed and was amazed that she could inspire such passion from so virile a man.

As Isis came down, Flare pulled his body free of hers. He ripped off the used condom and immediately donned another one. Isis rolled over onto her back and she saw his intent and nearly shouted with joy. Still on his knees, Flare pulled her to him. He guided her legs around him so that she straddled his cock and he entered her slowly, torturously, until they were completely joined.

Where before they had been wild with pleasure, now their desire was sweeter, gentler, and the ecstasy was even more intense than it had been before. Flare gently rocked his hips into hers, holding her tight against him as he filled her over and over. Isis' arms clutched at him tightly and she moaned softly with each movement their bodies made together. It was like a graceful dance, his thrust and retreat and the soft undulation of her hips as she accepted him over and over.

An hour later they were both panting and covered with slippery sweat. Still, they slowly rode themselves into oblivion. The pleasure was endless and all consuming. Isis hooked her ankles at the small of his back, changing the angle of their thrusts. They both choked out gasps at the new and amazing sensations awarded to them as a result.

Flare came first, groaning long and low and loud, rocking harder into her. Determined not to finish before Isis could orgasm, he rubbed her clit vigorously, thrusting harder and harder into her until she too was crying out her release.

When they came down they were both shaking. The room was at least eighty degrees and they were both covered in the sweat of their exertions. They clutched each other close, not even a breath separating them. They kissed long and deep, using lips and teeth and tongues to caress each other lovingly.

Tears leaked out of her eyes, mixing with her sweat, but they were tears of joy, not sorrow, and she rejoiced in that. She'd never felt so complete. So whole and right.

She loved him. It had been inevitable from their first kiss, Isis knew that now. She loved him more than life and couldn't imagine ever being without him again.

He'd made her feel normal and loved from the first. The pain she had held in her heart for so long had disappeared in his embrace. All the rage and despair she had learned to hide had been banished like ghosts, gone with the press of his lips on hers. Flare had stolen all of her pain away and replaced it with something clean and good and wonderful. How could she not love him?

They settled on the bed together—there was no need for covers, Flare was so hot and everything around them reflected that heat—and they lay beside each other, tracing their hands lazily over each other's bared skin.

Exhausted, Isis fell asleep tracing circles on the heavy muscles of Flare's chest.

* * * * *

When she awoke he was gone and the room had grown cold. But there was a note on the pillow next to her.

I'll be back tonight.

That was all it said. But it was more than enough for Isis. She hugged the note to her chest and rose from the enormous, soft bed. Finding her dress, she donned it as well as her discarded bra and panties once she had located them too. She wandered into the sitting room and looked around, still befuddled from her deep sleep.

She had never slept so much or so well as she had since meeting Flare.

Thirsty. She was thirsty. That was her first clear thought. Warily she approached the fireplace—it was crackling nicely and Isis realized Flare must have stoked it not long before he left. Isis stood on her tiptoes to reach the tall mantle and she found the box with the jewels encrusted on it. She opened it, took a small handful of the fl'shan powder and regarded the flames.

"Well, here goes nothing," she said aloud and threw the powder into the fire.

The flames flared dangerously hot before settling down again. "Um, I'd like something to drink," she said into the fire, feeling more than a little awkward.

There came a knock at the door.

"Damn, that was fast," she said with a frown, going to answer the door.

When she opened the door her jaw dropped. There was a man standing there. A seven-foot-tall man with a silver tray in one hand and a small smile playing about his shapely lips. He was a Shikar — there was no mistaking that same strength and magic Flare possessed and it seemed to hover about this man like a cloud.

"May I come in?" he asked and it seemed to Isis that this man rarely asked to do anything.

"Who are you?" she asked, stubbornly standing her ground even though the man was as intimidating as hell.

"You may call me Pulse. I am Flare's direct superior," he explained. His voice was beautiful, but it didn't make her feel at all like she did when listening to Flare.

"Come in." She stepped aside to allow him entry.

"I took the liberty of bringing you some food and drink to break your fast," the man said, walking into the sitting room as if he owned the place. He placed the silver tray on the coffee table and turned to look at her. "You are prettier than I expected," he said, but Isis couldn't tell by his tone if he was mocking or sincere.

"Flare isn't here," she told him.

"I did not come to see Flare," he said.

Isis frowned.

"I came to see you," he explained patiently.

"*Me*," Isis snorted. "Why?"

"Because I was curious about you." He took a deep breath and motioned for her to join him as he sat down. "I have heard much and I wanted to meet you firsthand."

"You've heard about me? From Flare?" She felt a small sense of betrayal that he would talk about her to someone else, but she reminded herself that his duty was to protect her and it was no doubt necessary that he report to someone of higher rank than he at some point.

Pulse smiled as if he knew what she was feeling. "We have other spies," he told her. His hair, black as pitch, sparkled with random tiny streaks of silver, as if he'd put them there carefully and on purpose.

Isis didn't know what to say.

"You needn't worry. I only know the bare facts of your life, not the dirty little secrets. At least...not all of them." He eyed her knowingly and she cringed inside at the thought of what he might actually know. "You're quiet interesting, for a human."

"How so?"

"For one, you deny your naturally sociable nature. You take care of yourself without the aid of family or loved ones. That is unusual in itself."

"No it isn't," she said. "A lot of people live like me. It's a lonely world out there."

Pulse sighed. "I also know that you're psychic," he said flatly, as if daring her to deny it.

"I'm learning new things about myself every day," she said with a lightheartedness she didn't feel.

"I heard that you killed a Daemon. With your bare hands."

Isis closed her eyes. When she opened them back up she noticed him studying her from head to toe. There was no passion in his gaze, only curiosity, so she did not take offense but still, his eyes — so like Flare's — made her uncomfortable. "I did. I don't know *how* I did," she added. "But Flare is sure he can teach me to control...well, whatever it was, so I'm looking forward to that."

"It's good that you are bonding so well with Flare."

Isis rolled her eyes. "What are you implying?"

"You are lovers."

"Yeah," she said flippantly. "Is there a rule against that?"

Pulse chuckled. "Actually there is, but Flare can explain that to you at a time of his own choosing. You needn't worry though, I approve of Flare's claim on you. I truly do," he assured her.

"Good," she said.

They eyed each other, sizing one another up like two generals ready to do battle, wills clashing.

For some strange and unexplainable reason she felt she could trust this man to the ends of the earth. He just seemed so...in control of everything around him. How she knew this, she couldn't have guessed, but knew it she did.

Taking a deep breath of courage, she took the plunge. "I wanted to meet with you too," she said.

Pulse's brows raised in surprise. "Really?" he asked musingly. "What about?"

"I heard that there are human women among you who fight the Daemons."

"Yes," Pulse nodded.

"I want to fight like they do. As Flare does. Before you say no," she hurried, "I can tell you that I'm physically strong enough, I know I'm brave enough and I can be loyal to a fault. I am capable of fighting. I know it. I just might need a little training first."

Pulse sat back with a smile. "Why do you wish to fight?"

"You want the truth?" she asked.

"Nothing but," he returned.

"Well," she started haltingly. "I've never really done anything with my life. After meeting and destroying a Daemon the other night I realized that I was capable of so much more than what I've been doing. I've just been wasting away all these years and I am ashamed to admit it, but it's true. I want to change things. I want to give my life a meaning. I think your cause is just and noble. I want to be a part of that."

"Have you talked to Flare about this idea of yours?"

Isis looked away from his all-too-knowing gaze. "No. But I'm sure I can convince him that this is right for me."

Pulse laughed. The sound was free and honest and welcoming. "I'm sure that if anyone can convince Flare it would be you."

"Would you be willing to let me join your army?"

Pulse leaned forward in his seat, his hair falling forward to obscure his features. "I would. You are indeed strong. And stubborn." His teeth flashed for a moment. "You need these traits to be part of our Alliance. Loyalty and obedience are key. Once you join with us there will be no turning back. Even if you and Flare break apart, you will still be required to serve as a warrior. Are you prepared for that?"

Isis felt a pure, blinding anguish at the thought of Flare leaving her—for she fully intended to stay with him for the rest of her life. She tamped down on the emotion, pushing the pain aside as she was used to doing.

But not before Pulse saw her reaction. "You love him," he said with a gentle smile.

Isis knew better than to lie to this man. He would see through her in a second, she was certain. And she wanted his approval—she really did. "He doesn't know," she answered painfully.

Pulse leaned back in his chair. "Your love is good. Hold on to that with all your might. It will make you strong for the hard times ahead."

"I want to be worthy of him," she said before she could stop the revealing confession.

"Then you should open yourself to him," he told her, his glowing eyes knowing far more than she was comfortable with. "Share yourself with him. Stop hiding behind a mask and make him your true mate for life."

"What if I can't get him to love me?" she asked in a choked whisper.

Pulse smiled at her tenderly. "I would not worry about that, my dear. Fate is fate and no one and nothing can stand against it."

"Fate," she mused.

"Do you believe in fate?" he asked curiously.

Isis thought for a long moment. "No," she said at last.

"Why not?" Pulse seemed truly puzzled.

"I don't know how to explain," she admitted.

"Try," Pulse commanded.

She took a deep breath and let it out in a whoosh. "I don't like to think that we were intended to suffer at fate's whim. I think we're just wandering around aimlessly, lost until we die. I have to think that."

"Your life has not been easy," he remarked.

"Easier than some, tougher than others," she evaded. "But my life has made me strong. Flare showed me that."

Pulse smiled again. "I am very glad that we had this talk, Isis." He rose and made to leave, abruptly cutting short their conversation.

"Wait," she called out, following him. "What do I do next? You said I could fight."

He turned to her. "And you will fight. But for now you needn't worry about that. Things will work themselves out, I am certain. Still, only time will tell." With that he nodded politely to her and walked out the door.

Chapter Ten

℘

When Flare entered the room Isis was waiting for him, sitting among the pillows of his bed and holding a dog-eared envelope in her hands. He came forward and kissed her, taking her breast in his hand to gently stroke it through the confines of her clothing. They parted, both breathless from the kiss, and regarded each other silently.

Isis had thought long and hard on Pulse's words. He'd seen that she hid a lot and had told her to open herself to Flare. This terrified her on many levels but at last she had come to a decision. And she truly felt it was the right one.

"You look lovely," Flare said.

"Thank you," she said, taking his hands in hers. "Sit down with me."

Flare did so, looking at her with a puzzled frown on his face.

"I'm ready to tell you my secret now," she said in a rush, eyeing him closely to judge his reaction. She thought she saw some relief there in his gaze.

"I will listen," he assured her with a nod of his head.

Isis took a deep breath but it did nothing to dispel the worry and pain that squeezed her heart. She untangled her fingers from his, knowing he could tell by the pulse in her wrist that something serious was about to come. But for a long moment she didn't know how to start. So, finally, she started at the beginning.

"A few months before I turned sixteen my stepfather started having long talks with me. He spent a lot of time with me. I liked it—at first. I didn't know him that well. He had been married to my mother for three years but we had never really had much to do with each other and I was glad for the sudden attention he was giving me.

"The talks eventually led to him fondling me, until we no longer talked at all. He just simply came into my room and let his hands roam all over me. He asked me, more than once, to feel him, to touch him back but I couldn't. I wouldn't. I knew what he was doing was wrong. But I thought fondling was all he would do. It wasn't.

"When I turned sixteen," Isis took another breath, "my stepfather raped me. The first time was horrible. I fought him and he hit me, over and over again, until I wasn't strong enough to struggle. I was covered in bruises the next day but my mother—who suffered from bipolar disorder—hit me often enough that she didn't even notice the new bruises and I didn't know how to tell her what had happened."

Isis couldn't look at him as she told the story. She didn't want to see his reaction. "After that, nothing happened for a couple of months. I thought that the horror was over, but of course it wasn't. My stepfather got away with it once and he knew he could get away with it again. So he raped me again one day after I came home from school—my sister and mother were out shopping together so we were alone.

"I had avoided being alone with him for two months. But I couldn't stop it from happening. I fought again, but he broke one of my ribs and I couldn't breathe, let alone fight. It was like my worst nightmares had come true. I was so scared. I didn't know what to do.

"I thought about telling my mother, of course. But my mother had no love for me. I look so much like my real father—who I never saw again after their divorce—that she hated me for the reminder of him.

"I so wanted to tell someone. Anyone. It was like pain and rage and shame were filling me up to the point of explosion. So I bought a journal and wrote down all that had been happening."

She glanced at Flare and almost swallowed her heart. She'd never seen anyone look so angry in her life. More than a little intimidated, she looked away again and continued before he could say anything.

"The better part of a year passed. My stepdad raped me, on average, every couple of months and it just got to where I didn't even bother fighting him anymore. I just laid there and took it and didn't tell anybody what was going on."

The temperature in the room was alarmingly high and growing hotter by the second.

"One afternoon I was doing my homework and my mom stormed into the room. 'What the hell is this?' she shrieked, waving my journal in my face, slapping me with it. How she'd found it, buried deep in my closet to keep it hidden, I'll never know. But she had found it and she had read it." Isis paused. "She didn't believe me," she whispered at last.

Isis trudged on, ignoring the intense heat baking off Flare. "I took a good beating from her that day. She was smaller than me, I could have fought her off, but I loved my mother. I don't blame her for the things she did to me because I know she was sick. But it was still a shock when she didn't believe the words I had written. I had envisioned my mother championing me over and over again, but when it came down to it, she just didn't believe me at all and so she beat me."

Isis wiped the sweat from her brow and reached for the glass of water on the nightstand. She drank a few sips before continuing. "My stepfather took every chance he could to tell me how no one anywhere would ever believe my story. He even convinced me of that. So I closed myself off from the world. I let go of all my friendships at school and I dropped out of all my extracurricular activities. When my stepfather was raping me I learned to leave my body, to let my mind just fly away from what was happening. It was the only thing that saved my sanity."

A teardrop landed on her hand and Isis put her fingers on her cheeks in surprise. She hadn't even realized she was crying. "Time passed. Things didn't change. Then one day, a few days after I'd turned seventeen, I came home early from school. I had a migraine — probably from all the stress I was under — and I had left school during one of our breaks. I didn't think anyone was home. I went to my room and started to do my homework when I heard some strange sounds.

"I thought someone was fighting. I could hear grunting and moaning. I followed the sound to my parents' bedroom. I didn't think about what I was doing — I had never been allowed in my parents' bedroom before—but I opened the door anyway and looked inside."

Isis' tears were falling fast now and there was nothing she could do to stem their flow. "My stepdad was having sex with my fifteen-year-old sister. At first I thought it was rape and something snapped inside me. I launched myself at him, throwing him from the bed. That crazy strength you saw in me the other night came out in me and I couldn't do anything to stop it. I pounded my stepfather's face into mush. I broke his nose, his jaw and I crushed his cheekbone before my sister pulled me off him. She was actually protecting him—can you believe that shit?"

She sniffed and was stunned when Flare gently offered her a soft, beige handkerchief. She took it gratefully and wiped her tears away. "My sister yelled at me that the sex had been completely consensual. I couldn't believe it. I told her so and she just laughed at me.

"'I'll fuck him better than you ever could,' she told me with this awful, sneering look on her face. I've never felt so much despair as I did when she said that to me. I lunged for my unconscious stepfather again but Maria got in the way. I couldn't stop myself in time. I hit her in the shoulder and broke it. She screamed and cried and I was mortified at what I had done, my blinding rage disappearing like a puff of smoke. Whether she liked me or not, she was my sister and I loved her. It killed me to know that I had hurt her.

"Needless to say, when my mother got home, I told her everything and once again she refused to believe me. But she couldn't ignore the condition of her husband and daughter—I had beaten them both—and this only made her angry as hell. So she told me to grab my stuff and go. She said she never wanted to see or hear from me again. I did as she said and left my old life behind that very night.

"I lived out of my car at first. I quit school so I could work to get a roof over my head, and I spent each day in a daze of shock. This went on for about four months until I saw my sister and stepdad in the mall one afternoon. They were holding hands and going into Victoria's Secret—that's a lingerie store, by the way, in case you didn't know. They were laughing and happy. My stepdad's face was still bruised in places and I know for certain he'd had to have reconstructive surgery to fix his cheekbone. Watching them together that way did something to me. I didn't let them see me. I just left and went out to my car."

Isis met Flare's gaze and it was so hot with rage it could have burned the clothes from her body. "I sat in my car for about an hour, just thinking about my life and what I needed to do to change it. To forget the pain my family had caused me. I cranked my car and left the state—I didn't even gather my stuff first. I just drove until I ran out of gas money. I took odd jobs, never making any friends of course—I hurt too much for that. Sometimes I lived in my car, other times I would rent small places to stay in for a while until the money became so tight I had to leave again. I lived that way for many years. Running from my past, yet haunted by it all the time."

Isis laughed ironically. "One day I just decided that the best way for me to make money was by using my body. But not for prostitution—that I couldn't ever have done, no matter how desperate times became for me. I got a job at The Pink Pit and worked every night until I started to gain a following. The money was good from the beginning, but it kept rolling in and I kept on earning it. It was the best job I'd ever had.

"That was the longest I've ever stayed in one place since I left home," she admitted. "Though I've tried, I can't rationalize why I'm still so traumatized by my past life. I just am. The pain of my memories makes me a little crazy sometimes. I fight it, but I just can't escape it.

"I've always kept my addresses and phone numbers secret because I didn't want there to ever be a chance that my family might try to find me and succeed. But then, last week, this note came to my P.O. box." She handed him the letter her sister had written.

Flare studied the envelope for a moment then pulled the sheet of paper out. He read it in silence and Isis remembered the words as clearly as if *she* held the note and not him.

Dearest sister,

Just thought you'd like to know that Dad...I mean Jeff...and I are getting married. I'm pregnant with our first child, isn't that lovely?

Mom died cursing your name. I'm sure you didn't know that, so I'm glad to tell you. Toward the end all she could talk about was how much she hated you. Hated that you even came from her blood. She never once believed you, you realize that? She never even suspected anything between me and Jeff either. It was so much fun to mess around behind her crazy-ass back! Ah, I almost miss those days.

We don't miss you around here though. I certainly never have. But I knew I just had to tell you my happy news. See, I told you I could satisfy him more than you. Now he's all mine. If the world is kind you'll be so jealous you won't know what to do. I'm betting that you'll just cry like a baby and retreat into whatever little hole you've wriggled your way into. You were always such a wuss.

Anyway, things are going great for us. We fuck like bunnies and with Mom gone now we don't even have to hide it anymore, isn't that great? I hope things are terrible for you and that this letter hurts the hell out of you.

Your loving sister,
Maria

"How you have suffered," he whispered, voice unsteady. Hands shaking with rage, Flare crumpled the letter in his hand. Isis cried out and reached for it, but he held it beyond her reach. He eyed her stonily. "You will never read this shit again," he told her. *"Never!"* He gritted the words out.

"It's the only letter I have from my family," she said.

"And it will be the only one you ever get. Isis, why do you punish yourself by keeping this horrible thing close to you?"

"I don't know," she admitted with a sob.

Flare eyed her knowingly, a fierce rage simmering below the surface of his gaze. "You blame yourself for how your sister turned out."

Isis shook her head, knowing the lie for what it was.

"You *do*," he insisted. "I know you. You're thinking that if you had done something—anything—differently, you might have changed things. But don't you see, Isis, there was never anything you could do. You were only a child and you were alone."

"Maybe if I had gone to my mother in person, picked a time when she was calm, maybe if she hadn't read my journal, she would have believed my words instead."

Flare's jaw was clenched tight. "Your mother was mad. Nothing could have saved your sister. She didn't want to be saved. There was absolutely nothing you could have done to change things."

"I don't believe that," she admitted.

"Then I will teach you to believe it," Flare said, beyond rage. He ripped up the letter and envelope and tossed the bits of paper about the room. "This never happened," he said.

"You can't change the past," she told him.

"No you can't. But you *can* forget. You can fill your life with such love and laughter and wonder that your memories will fly away like dust in the wind. You never have to think about this horror again."

Isis bowed her head and looked at her hands. They were clenched into tight fists, her nails cutting her palms. She deliberately relaxed them. "I have thought of something that might help me do that," she said cautiously.

Flare lifted her head up with a gentle hand beneath her chin. "What is that?"

Her gaze met his. "I want to be a warrior. Like you."

Chapter Eleven

ഇ

"Before you say no," she rushed before he could respond, "hear me out, okay?"

Flare sat back a little and motioned for her to continue.

"I'm strong—you've shown me that. You can teach me to become stronger. I can fight the Daemons alongside you just like Cady and the other human women do. I'm not afraid. And I want to be a part of something important for once in my life."

"What you ask is difficult. I would have to ask my superior—"

"Oh, I've already asked him," she broke in, unconcerned.

Flare's eyes went wide. "The Generator was here? *Today*?" he asked with shock.

Isis frowned. "The Generator? I don't know what you mean. He said his name was Pulse."

"Pulse?" he said, dumbfounded. "He's never asked me to call him by his true name," he mused as if more to himself than her.

"He and I already talked about it. Pulse says I can join your army, become a fighter for your cause."

Flare's eyes blazed. "You talked of this to him before you talked to me?"

"Well, I figured I should, since I was given the opportunity. He is your superior officer or whatever. I'd have to ask him eventually."

"What else did you speak of?" he asked in a tight voice.

"Not much else. He just asked me a few questions and then left. It was a really brief visit, thank goodness. He's really...intimidating," she admitted with a short laugh.

"Perhaps. Yet you could trust him to the ends of the Earth," Flare said loyally, echoing her earlier thoughts. It was obvious by the tone in his voice that he greatly admired Pulse.

Eyeing her in such a way that Isis couldn't guess at his thoughts, Flare asked in a deceptively gentle tone, "Did you speak of *anything* else?"

"No," she assured him.

Flare watched her carefully for a moment then nodded his head. "Are you sure about wanting to be a warrior?"

"Absolutely," Isis said, definitively relieved that he wasn't arguing with her about her decision. "But I'll need your help with that. I don't really know what to do."

"I will guide you always," he promised. "You can count on that."

Isis looked at him, studying the planes of his handsome face. She'd thought this moment would bring fear and uncertainty, but it did not. She had never been surer of herself. "I love you," she admitted softly, taking the plunge.

A halo of flame appeared around his head and his eyes reflected the heat of that fire. The temperature in the room soared until the very air was almost too thick to breathe. "Say that again," he told her, his voice thick and rough. His gaze locked with hers and refused to let go. He reached for her, taking her into his arms. "Say it again." He repeated his command into the curve of her neck and shoulder.

"I love you, Flare." His skin was so hot as he held her, but Isis welcomed the heat. It proved to her that she had definitely gotten his attention with her admission.

"Oh, Isis, *baby*," he said and claimed her mouth with his, tightening his arms about her.

Flare lowered her back onto the bed, kissing her so deeply that he stole her very breath away and gave his own in return. Tasting him, she ran her tongue alongside his, sucking on it gently. His flavor was wild, swamping her senses and making her reel like a drunkard in his arms. She took his full bottom lip between her teeth and tugged gently, playfully.

Growling, Flare let one of his Foils come out of the tip of his finger. It was glowing red hot and sharper than any sword. Taking great care, he traced his Foil down her front, slicing her dress, bra and panties so that her clothes fell away instantly. The frayed edges of the clothing were smoking and Flare pulled them away from her completely, tossing the ruined material to the floor.

He turned back to her, seeing her glorious nudity and nearly coming undone from the beautiful image. He tamped down on his raging need and put his hot lips on hers once again, letting his hands wander freely over her, concentrating on her breasts, belly and labia until she was moaning uncontrollably into his mouth and writhing beneath him.

"You are the most amazing female I have ever known," he told her, holding her gaze with his. His fingers unerringly found her clit and toyed with it tenderly as he looked down at her. "I can't imagine how I've managed to live without you for so long," he whispered in admission. "I can never let you go now. You *know* that, don't you?"

"I'll never let you go," she sighed. "And I'd kill anyone and anything who dared to try to come between us."

Unable to stop himself, Flare laughed at her words. She sounded deadly serious, and for some reason that made him feel joyous. He kissed her mouth hard and rose to remove his own clothing with impatient hands. He donned a condom in record time, with trembling hands.

Once he was nude, he came down on top of her once again, gently, so as not to hurt her. "By Grimm, your skin feels so *soft*," he murmured, kissing her temples, cheeks and chin with light presses of his shapely lips.

"And you're so hard," Isis said wickedly before taking his thick cock in her hand.

Flare caught his breath at the caress. When her fingers began to move on him, stroking every inch of him, he growled and took her nipple into his mouth to tease and titillate her as she was doing to him. Isis let her free hand fist at the hair on the nape of his neck, her fingers tangling in his soft hair, holding him to her breast.

Her hold on him tightened and he cried out his passion. His fingers dug into the mattress at her sides, leaving singe marks in the sheets as he lost some of his control. "Baby, you drive me wild." He let his lips tickle her nipple as he spoke the words before he flicked out his tongue and tasted her again. He pulled himself from her grasp, ignoring her murmur of disappointment. It was necessary, however, for his control was slipping fast beneath her caress.

Holding her gaze captive with his, he pressed into her. The large, mushroom head of his cock stretched her tender flesh and she cried out as it popped into her unexpectedly. Never letting go of her gaze, he moved his hands down between their bodies and found her clit. He let his fingers gather her moisture so that they were slippery over her tight, erect flesh.

Isis melted around him. He sank into her, filling her completely. When he reached the heart of her, fully sheathed, they both moaned, yet never did they stop gazing into each other's souls. His hair fell forward like a dark curtain, tangling with hers. With his free hand, Flare caught one of hers and held it back against the mattress, entwining their fingers so that they were joined in every way.

He began to rock into her. Gently at first. So gently that he brought tears to her eyes. Then with deeper, surer strokes that made her gasp and writhe. All the while his hand in hers held it back against the bed, and his other toyed with her hard little clit. He left no part of her unclaimed, laying waste to all of her secrets, fears and misgivings. She was totally his.

Isis couldn't find a breath that wasn't thick with his scent and heat, nor did she want to. He swamped all of her senses, making her feel open and free, yet cared for and protected in ways she'd never experienced before. In that moment he could have claimed her soul and she wouldn't have minded in the least.

With long, sure, gentle strokes of his body sliding into hers, he drove her up high to the heavens. She came softly, easily, tightening her body around his until he too joined her at passion's peak. They cried out together, gazes still locked on each other's, so that they saw the magic working in their eyes as they came together.

Several minutes later, Flare collapsed onto the bed beside her. "By Grimm, but you have drained me, woman," he said with harsh gasps. Then he turned to her and kissed her gently on the mouth. "You astound me at every turn," he murmured. They eyed each other for long minutes, each content within themselves.

"I want you to teach me to be as strong as you are," she whispered abruptly, fingers stroking his cheek softly.

Flare smiled at her tenderly. "You already are. But," he continued softly, gaze growing thoughtful, yet worried, "there is one thing you could do to become even stronger."

Interest piqued, Isis felt her eyes go wide. "What?"

"It won't be easy," he explained.

"I'm willing to do anything," she vowed.

"You could become a Shikar," he told her softly.

Isis frowned, confused. "What?"

"I can change you into what I am," he told her patiently. "You can have the same traits as we Shikars do. But...as I said, it won't be easy."

"How can you do that?"

"You have noticed that I always use a condom when we mate," he remarked and Isis nodded. "We Shikars have a rule among us, one that is virtually unbreakable. We cannot lie with human women without protection."

"Why?" she asked, puzzled.

"Because our seed, spent inside a woman's body, would kill her."

Isis gasped. "You could do this? Kill me with your sperm?"

Flare shook his head. "You are one of the very rare human women who could possibly overcome your death and be reborn as a Shikar."

Isis eyed him thoughtfully. "So what you're saying is, you think you can change me, but there is no guarantee that I won't die trying."

"Yes." He watched her carefully to witness her reaction. "Four human women have been changed. No more. But you and I love each other, and you are strong. I believe I could change you. I wouldn't risk your life without being sure."

"You love me?" she asked in a whisper.

Flare's gaze could have burned stone, it was so hot. "I do."

Isis felt a thrill of exaltation. Calming herself with some effort, she thought on his words. She looked back at her life, seeing how empty it had been before Flare, how dark and cold and lonesome her world had been before meeting him. The thought of a future with him at her side, a future that would let her live as long as he could, be as strong as he was, was scary yet at the same time savagely exciting.

She made her decision almost immediately. "Okay," she said, rolling on top of him. "Change me then," she whispered against his mouth before kissing him long and deep. Her nimble fingers sought and found the tip of his used condom and she pulled it off him easily, tossing it over her shoulder carelessly. Isis then moved down his body and took him into her mouth before he could even voice a protest.

Not that he would have. Her mouth was like magic on him. Isis used her lips, teeth and tongue to tease and torment him. Then she shocked him by stretching her mouth around him and deep-throating his erection. He felt the silken heat of her suckling him and bucked uncontrollably against her.

"Wait," he said, pushing her back. Isis moaned around his cock then slowly released him. Before she could ask why, he turned her body so that they were in the sixty-nine position. This opened her wide to accept Flare's kiss, making her feel vulnerable and yet strong at the same time.

She took him in her mouth again as he licked the seam of her pussy, delving in deeper to taste her. Isis moaned around his cock and she felt the vibration of his answering moan against her wet, aching cunt. He flicked his tongue against her clit, driving her wild so that she suckled him in response, bobbing her head up and down his length.

When his tongue slid over her anus she choked on a cry of pure ecstasy. She stroked his legs then let her hands wander, at last cupping his testicles gently in her eager palm. She stroked him there as she stroked his cock with her mouth, and she felt him growl against her, licking her anus once again in reward for her sensual ministrations.

At last, he could take no more. He turned her again, her mouth making a popping sound as it released him, until he had settled her on her knees and moved up behind her. He immediately thrust into her tender, pink cunt. They both cried out with pleasure, and he withdrew only to plunge back inside her welcoming body.

"You are so wet," he growled. "So sweet and tight."

Isis gasped. "You're so hard and big. I *love* your cock," she moaned.

He thrust into her, hard, then took a deep, calming breath. "I've never wanted anyone the way I want you," he revealed.

"You make me feel whole," she admitted in return, then moaned as his hands squeezed the cheeks of her ass.

"I want to be one with you forever, just like this." He thrust again, hitting the mouth of her womb hard so that they both gasped.

Then there was no more room for words. The only sounds in the room were the rasps of their heavy breathing and the wet, sucking sounds her body made with every thrust and withdrawal of his. Flare's hands moved around her and took her bouncing breasts in his hands. His clever fingers squeezed and pinched her nipples, wringing a cry from her as the pleasure hit her like a physical blow.

"Come for me, baby," he commanded her. "Milk me with your sweet pussy."

His words enflamed her as much as his touch. He pounded into her, increasing his pace and strength, and then she was flying. Isis heard herself scream as the climax slammed into her. Her whole body trembled, her mind went blank and she was filled with such exquisite sensations that she nearly passed out.

Flare let her come down and regain her senses. He still thrust in and out of her wet, clinging body, but softer now. "When I come, think only of me. Hold onto your love for me in your mind and heart," he instructed breathlessly. "I will follow you into death and save you. But you must fight the urge to travel on into oblivion before I reach you."

Isis felt her passion rise again—she couldn't help it. He was still moving inside of her and the sound of his voice alone was a caress. He thrust into her harder, faster, and she cried out as yet another climax hit her hard. She heard Flare's shout of triumph and the scalding hot splash of his cum spurted deep into her.

Chapter Twelve

ஐ

For a moment, everything was fine. They both came down from their high and collapsed into the mattress. Their breathing slowed eventually and the air grew cooler.

Then, without warning, her body temperature fell alarmingly. Her head ached like a migraine had taken hold. "It's so cold," she whispered in wonder as bright starbursts lit within her eyes.

"Hold onto me!" Flare clutched her body to his.

"So...cold..." She felt the darkness coming to swallow her up and felt a jolt of real fear. But she tamped down on that fear and rallied her strength. She fought against the lure of death, struggled for her very life, fighting as she never had before. "Flare," she called out weakly.

Isis heard his echoing words as he called to her. She felt a slipping sensation, as if she were dangling from a high cliff and was too weak to hold on with her tired hands. There was a wrenching feeling as she fell and she knew her soul had broken free of her body.

Darkness blinded her. All her senses fled, save one. She could still hear Flare calling for her. For one seemingly endless moment she wondered why she should stay behind when the still call of death was so strong. It was so hard to fight the deepening dark.

Then she felt Flare's presence, there in the blackness, strengthening her waning resolve to live. He called her name again—his voice sounding miles away—and she tried to call back, but she had no voice with which to speak. She tried to find him but she had no sight with which to see.

"Isis!" Flare's voice seemed closer.

With a strength that surprised her in this dark place, she pulled away from the lure of oblivion. She fought to take hold of her own soul, fought to guide it back from the precipice of death.

"I'm here, Isis." There was a falling sensation again as she slowly became aware of her physical body once more. She was cradled in Flare's warm arms, lifeless and spent. But her will was strong and she forced the weakness away. She felt her soul enter her body with a slamming, brutal force that made her scream and then she fainted in Flare's embrace.

Moments later she came to herself again and heard an astonishing sound. Flare was weeping, calling her name over and over again. Isis sat up dizzily and Flare gasped. He held her closer and all the cold she'd felt before was banished with his endless heat. She met his gaze with her own and saw the tears he had wrought for her.

Flare ran his hand over her head, stroking her hair. "I thought I'd lost you," he managed in a gravelly voice, swallowing his tears.

"I'm fine," she croaked and her throat hurt as if she'd been shouting. Isis cleared her throat and tried again. "I'm okay. Really." Her hands came up and brushed away the last of his tears. "I'm feeling stronger now." She sat up in his arms and looked around her.

Everything had changed. Colors were brighter, scents were stronger and she felt sure she could hear the squeak of a mouse from half a mile away if she wanted. Her body felt strong—stronger than she'd ever felt before. Ever. She looked down at herself, expecting something—anything—that would reveal the depth of her transformation. But she looked the same as far as she could tell and almost felt a pang of disappointment.

Flare unerringly knew what she was thinking. "Your eyes have changed," he said, still stroking her hair tenderly.

"How do you mean?" she asked.

"Go and look." He pointed toward the mirror mounted on a far wall. Isis rose and approached it with some small trepidation. She had to stand up on her tiptoes to look into the mirror and when she did she gasped. Her eyes looked exactly like Flare's, golden yellow with a rim of fiery orange around the dark pupil.

"I have Shikar eyes," she said in wonder. "Did it work then? Am I a Shikar?" She had to be sure.

Flare nodded, coming to stand behind her so that their images overlapped each other in the mirror. "You are a Shikar. You have been gifted with longevity, super speed, strength and intelligence. You are no longer a human woman."

"I had super strength already," she joked, but she felt no humor at all in the situation. All she could feel was awe.

"You will be even stronger now," he told her. "I wonder what Caste you will be?" he mused quietly.

"Caste?"

"Your class of distinction within our world. I am a multiple Caste, as I have told you. But multiple Castes are not common. You will likely have one skill that is powerful above all others, and your Caste will be set by whatever that skill may be."

"You mean I might be able to make fire like you?" she asked in astonishment.

"It is a possibility," he allowed. "It is clear you will not be a Traveler. Travelers' eyes are black throughout. But there are still many Castes, some of them well known while others are entirely unique. My superior — Pulse — is known as The Generator. He can create and control lightning and that is a rare Caste indeed — no one else in our history has ever possessed such power. You could have any number of new skills. But it may take some time before we know what you are capable of."

Isis laughed joyously and threw her arms around him. "You're the best thing that has ever happened to me," she told him with a smile and kissed him hard. Then she turned once more to the mirror, marveling at her strange new eyes. "I'm a Shikar." She tried it out, feeling the excitement and impatience of the thought of what tomorrow would bring her. "I can't believe it," she said, clapping her hands and bouncing on her feet excitedly.

"Come," he took her hand with a grin. "Let's rest. You've been through a lot today."

"But I'm not tired."

"Then *try* to rest," he answered with a show of patience in the face of her exuberance.

Isis shook her head. "I was hoping we could go back to the hotel and find my things. My car I don't care about, but I have a picture of my mother in one of my bags and I don't want to lose it."

"Your belongings may no longer be there," he pointed out.

"If they aren't, I'll just ask the desk clerk where they are and threaten police involvement if they don't find my stuff—that motel is just seedy enough that I believe they'd do whatever it takes to avoid the law." Isis went to Flare's armoire herself and rummaged through the strange, alien clothes she found there.

Isis held up a black tunic for him to see. "What material is this?" she asked curiously.

"I don't know its name, but it is fireproof. Most of my clothes are. I'd burn a lot of material if they weren't and I doubt our seamstresses would be happy with me for that."

"Help me find some clothes," she urged.

Flare came between her and the armoire, sorting through the clothing until he came up with a brown tunic that would be as long as a dress on her. "This is all I have for now. We'll get you some more clothes as soon as we return."

"Once I get my stuff I won't need them," she said, donning the tunic then watching as he too dressed. In black from head to toe, his hair shining indigo in the dim light, he reached out for her hand.

"Are you ready?" he asked.

Isis knew he meant to Travel. She took a deep breath and nodded her head yes. "Let's do this."

One instant they were in Flare's room and the next they were standing in a completely ruined hotel room. All of Isis' things were tossed about and the bed had been shredded, springs littering the floor. The walls looked as if a strong wind would crumple them. Isis stepped out of the room and saw that the rest of the hotel was in similar shape and was completely deserted. "Damn. This place looks worse than it did before," she remarked. "Did the Daemons do all of this?"

"Get your things quickly," he warned her, already gathering up a handful of her underwear and stuffing it into one of her bags.

Isis moved back into the room and found a pair of jeans, a T-shirt and some modest cotton underwear. Grabbing a pair of tennis shoes, she went into the bathroom, closing the door softly behind her as Flare continued his swift packing. Isis used the toilet and washed her hands and face. Then she ran her fingers through her hair, working out the tangles as best she could.

Looking at her reflection in the vanity mirror, she was once more astonished by her transformation. She simply couldn't resist staring at her new, alien eyes in wonder.

Isis put her hands up before her face, studying them carefully for any differences she hadn't yet noticed. She looked the same as always. Curious, she slammed her hands down on the sink.

The sink broke off the wall and fell to the floor.

"What was that?" Flare immediately demanded through the door.

"It's okay," she called back hurriedly, looking down with shock at the devastation she had caused with one easy blow. "The sink just fell." She didn't tell him how.

Isis took off Flare's tunic and donned her own far more familiar clothing. She was lacing up the tennis shoes when she felt something strange. It was as if someone was massaging part of her brain with feathers and a stifling, heavy weight seemed to press down on her chest. Her skin felt stretched and thin over her bones and her heartbeat rapidly sped up. This alien feeling alarmed her for she knew instinctively that it wasn't a good sign.

"Flare," she called, looking about for a weapon. She grabbed a plumbing pipe from the mess she'd made of the sink and tested its weight in her hand. Satisfied that it would make a good tool, she clutched it tight in her hand.

"What is it?" Flare asked. "There is concern in your voice."

He read her so well. "I don't feel right. I think something bad is about to happen," she called, stepping out of the bathroom cautiously. She hurried to help Flare pack the rest of her things, finding the dog-eared photo of her mother in her younger days and putting it in her back pocket for safe keeping.

Seconds later the feelings Isis was experiencing intensified alarmingly. There was definitely something wrong. "I feel so weird," she told Flare.

He looked at her immediately. "How so?" he asked, concerned.

"My brain is all tingly and it feels like a Doberman is sitting on my chest. Plus my stomach hurts and my skin feels weird."

Flare grabbed her bags. "Come on," he urged hurriedly.

"What does it mean?" She had to ask.

"You are sensing a Daemon. Maybe more than one, judging by the strength of your feelings. We have to leave. Now."

Isis reached out to take his hand, preparing to Travel.

A Daemon appeared in the littered room. Roaring, it rushed them and swiped out at Isis with one clawed hand. Isis moved faster than she ever had before, ducking out of the way of the blow just in time to save her skin. But another Daemon had entered the room without her seeing it and when she moved away from the first monster, she tripped into the second one. This Daemon caught her arm and tugged. If she'd been any weaker her shoulder would have dislocated instantly.

The feel of the creature's skin on hers was repulsive and horrific. Its claws dug into her arms, tearing her skin and making her bleed. Isis cried out and turned to face it, jerking away at the last second and raising the pipe in her hand high over her head. She brought it down with all the strength she could muster, screaming in a sudden, blinding rage.

The pipe sank down deep into bone and sinew. She had crushed the monster's head...but it still grabbed out for her with a roar that threatened to shatter her eardrums.

"Take its heart," Flare told her as he quickly took care of the first Daemon. His hands were already in its chest cavity, even as the beast beat him with its giant claws.

Isis took one more swipe at the thing's devastated skull, tearing half the head off with her blow. She threw the pipe down and screamed a war cry as she launched herself at the monster.

Something happened, something unexpected. Long, blue-white glowing blades seemed to spring forth from the bones of her knuckles and before she knew what to do about them, she had sunk them deep into the monster's trunk.

The creature was tall. Isis used her strange blades to walk up the beast's body so that she could better fight for its heart. Then she took one strong swipe with the blades, tearing a long gash in its chest as easily as she might have swatted at a fly. Through all the gore that was gushing out of the ruined beast's body, Isis saw the great, beating heart of the vile creature. She grabbed it and ripped it free with a horrible, wet wrenching sound that almost made her gag. "Holy shit," she screamed and fell back away from the beast.

Flare came up behind her and grabbed the heart away from her. Instantly the still beating organ surged into flames. The monster fell back, a gurgling sound coming from its ruined head, dead the moment it hit the floor. Flare threw the ashes of the heart away and made sure he had Isis' attention.

"Do you see this?" A small, round ball of flame floated above his hand. He turned his hand this way and that, rolling it like a quarter between his fingers. Isis watched in fascination as he turned to the beast's body, the ball of flame growing from golf ball size to basketball size immediately. Flare threw the ball of fire at the creature and its body cooked in the flame. "If you want we can try to see if you can do this too," he told her. But Isis was doubtful that she'd ever be able to do the magic he did so easily.

The hotel room was full of smoke, but with her new eyes, Isis easily saw her way around. Both she and Flare moved at once, grabbing her scattered bags one last time before meeting in the center of the room, instantly entwining their hands. "Let's get the fuck outta here," she said.

The ruined room disappeared and they Traveled back home together.

Chapter Thirteen

ဢ

The first thing they did when they returned to Flare's apartment was take a bath in the great sunken tub. Together. First they scrubbed each other to get clean then they drained the dirty water and replaced it with hot, clean water, adding an herbal-smelling soap to create bubbles. Isis settled back against her mate with a heartfelt sigh. Flare cradled her in his arms as he healed her minor injuries with tender, thorough care.

"Did you see what happened?" she asked, looking at him over her shoulder through the wet curtain of her hair.

Flare brushed some of the wet strands off her face. "When?" he asked.

"When those things came out of my hands and I creamed that monster."

"Those are your Foils. I suspect that you'll have no problem learning how to control them." Flare chuckled, as if looking forward to watching her try.

"So you think maybe I'll be a Foil Caste?" she asked curiously.

Flare shook his wet head. "I can't be sure. I don't think so. It's clear that you're a strong Hunter—I didn't even sense the Daemons until you told me what you were feeling. We can't be sure yet what you'll be."

Isis felt the hard, thick weight of his cock pressing against her back. She turned in the water, straddled him and immediately took him deep into her body, coming down fully upon his thick girth. Flare gasped and clutched at her as she began to ride him.

"Slow down," he moaned, but Isis was already fast approaching her orgasm and she didn't want to stop the wonderful sensations flooding through her from head to toe.

Her hands brought him close as she kissed him with all the passion in her soul. His fingers dug into the soft skin of her ass as he helped her to bob up and down on his rampant cock. They both gasped into each other's mouths every time she came down upon him, sheathing him completely within her eager body.

The tips of her nipples scraped deliciously against the muscled ridge of his chest. The caress made her nipples as hard as tiny little diamonds, and her breasts felt heavy against him. An ache had started deep within her and she knew she would come soon. But not before she told him what she wanted to say.

"I love the way you laugh," she told him. "You don't do it often enough."

"I've laughed more with you these past days than I've laughed in a long time," he admitted.

She ran her hands up and down his thick, muscular arms. "I love the way you're always so gentle with me." He started to say something but she shushed him with a finger on his shapely lips, moving her hips in a way that stole his breath away. "I love the way you're always so strong and dependable. I love how noble and loyal you are to your cause, how proud and formidable a warrior you are. And I love *you*. I'm crazy about you."

"You make me feel strong," he said, surging into her over and over. "I feel I am the luckiest being alive—I have your passion and your love and I did not know it but I *needed* those things from you. Only you. You will never know just how desperately I need you."

"Show me," she said, rising to offer him her breast. He took her nipple into his mouth and suckled her, their wet bodies sliding deliciously against one another. The sounds of the waves they made in the tub lulled them. They slowed their vigorous pace and savored the moment.

"Oh, Isis, you make me feel such wonderful things," he moaned and clutched her tight, moving to her other breast to suckle and tease.

Isis let her head fall back. Flare's mouth moved from her breast to her exposed throat. He took her skin in his mouth, suckling, nibbling, leaving a dark mark behind. His mark of possession and desire, clear for anyone to see.

"I want to steal all your pain," he said, claiming her mouth.

They kissed, lips, teeth and tongues coming into play. The kiss stole her breath away and filled her with a fire that blazed hot and eager. "You've already done that," she gasped for breath, amazed that it was the truth.

There was no more room for words. Mindless with her pleasure, she rode him faster and harder until they were both moaning uncontrollably. He filled her so tightly, so fully, that tears leaked out of the corners of her eyes.

He slammed into her hard and she saw stars. She was close. So close. Flare's nimble fingers moved between them and unerringly found her clit. It was swollen and aching and he stroked little circles around it, making it more and more erect. He rolled the tiny nubbin of flesh between his fingertips and she screamed, coming instantly.

Flare felt her body milking his, but he kept an iron-hard control on his urge to spend himself then and there. He had so much more planned for her before he could find his own release.

When she collapsed bonelessly into his embrace, he pulled himself free of her. With gentle care he turned her, urging her to brace her hands on the end of the tub. She was bent over before him, showing him all of her secrets. The vision of her pink, wet flesh made him weak with desire. He couldn't control himself. He bent down and kissed her, pressing his lips firmly to her anus.

Isis cried out and surged up, but Flare pushed her back down with his hand, holding her captive there as he loved her. His tongue darted out to taste her and the flavor was of the fragrant bathwater. With his right index finger he penetrated her there, wringing a choked gasp from Isis' lips.

Thrusting his finger in and out of her, he felt her body relax around him. He put another finger into her, stretching her, and her whole being shivered and quaked beneath his ministrations. She was moaning repeatedly now, climbing high toward another release. Flare pulled his fingers free of her body and positioned himself behind her.

The feel of his cock stretching the tender flesh of her anus was mind-boggling. It felt as if she were being penetrated by a baseball bat. He was so big. So thick and long. Isis had no idea how he was going to fit there.

But fit he did. Slowly but surely, he sank deeper into her. The mushroom head of his sex popped past her sphincter and he was in. Isis' breath sobbed out of her. He filled her deeper and deeper until he was seated almost to the hilt. Flare placed his hands on her hips, pulling her back against him. He reached with one hand and thrust his fingers deep inside of her soaking wet pussy. He stroked her there and began to ride her ass gently.

Increasing the pace and force of his thrusts gradually kept Isis from feeling any pain at all with this wicked possession. Her body felt stretched tight, he filled her so fully, but it was a delicious, welcome feeling. The feel of his fingers playing with her pussy only added to her pleasure. She felt her body reflexively tighten on his as he brushed the sensitive nub of her clit and they both moaned. Flare waited for her body to relax again then began his thrusts once more.

Flare was dizzy with pleasure. She was so tight it stole his breath away. Her body was silken, slippery wet and cool against his rising body heat. He knew if he wasn't careful that he'd have the water boiling with the heat of his uncontrollable passion. Flare already knew his cock was hot enough to singe, buried deep inside of her, but Isis seemed to like that sensation so he let himself stay warm inside of her.

When Isis came, it was with a broken scream. Her body, racked with shudders, opened fully to him. He seated himself to the hilt and let go of his iron control.

He cried out, unable to keep the sound muffled, and thrust hard. Her body milked his and he was lost. He shouted his triumph as he shot his scalding hot cum deep within her. Spurting over and over, he filled her until his juices leaked out between them. Isis gave one last cry and went limp beneath him.

They slid back into the water, breathless, mindless. Flare left her body and they both groaned as he popped free of her. They fell away and stroked each other's bodies freely, more to soothe now than to titillate, hands gentle and undemanding.

"Oh my God, I never thought I'd do anything like that," she said breathlessly.

"Did you like it?" he asked gently.

"Holy shit, I *loved* it!" she said at once. "That was the most incredible sensation I've ever felt."

"Good," he grunted and lifted her against him. He rose with her in his arms and set her down on the tile outside the tub. Stepping out of the bath, Flare grabbed a super-soft towel and rubbed her dry. When he was done, she took the towel from him and made to dry him off but he shook his head at her with a cocksure smile.

Fire consumed his form. Isis gasped and stepped back reflexively. A short second passed, heat baking off him, then the flame died down, disappearing as quickly as it had appeared. When she could see past the spots blurring her vision she saw that Flare was completely dried from head to toe.

"That's not fair," she said, hair still wet and dripping down her back.

Flare laughed and reached for her once again. He swung her up into his arms and carried her like a baby into his bedroom. He placed her gently back among the plush pillows and lay down beside her, his hands immediately gathering her close, spooning with her.

"We'll have to move," he told her idly. "I have claimed you. I am no longer a bachelor."

"That's cool," she said, resting her hands on her naked tummy.

He was silent for long moments and she wondered what he was thinking. She didn't have to wait long to find out.

"I am going to the Territories tomorrow to kill your stepfather," he admitted softly at the nape of her neck.

Isis stiffened and pulled away from him. "No. *Fuck* no. He's not worth it. He's just a big fat loser. A nobody. Killing him won't solve anything."

"It would make us both feel better," he pointed out stubbornly.

"I can't let you do that," she told him.

The temperature in the room soared as heat wafted off him. "He dared to touch you. To hurt you. To break you. I cannot and will not let him go unpunished for that."

"Just leave it alone," she said.

"I cannot believe that you are defending him," he remarked angrily.

Isis sighed heavily and met his hot gaze with hers. "I'm not defending him. And if you'd offered to kill him two weeks ago I would have said yes right away. But I know you. You protect humans all the time. You could never willingly kill one."

"I could very easily kill him," Flare gritted the words out. "He deserves to die for what he did to you."

"Don't," she said. "Let's just forget about him forever. We don't ever have to think about my past again. You've seen to that. You've given me a wonderful future to look forward to. You fixed me, made me whole. Killing my stepdad would only open the old wounds for me." She grinned at him impishly. "Besides, you don't know how to find him."

Flare grunted but said nothing. He reached for her again and captured her in his embrace. He spooned with her, stroking his hands all over the front of her body. Despite how tired she was, Isis still responded to his caresses. His cock was hard at her back and she was growing wet again. But nature took over and her exhaustion caught up to her with a bang. She went to sleep with the feel of him fondling her breasts.

Her dreams were the sweetest she'd ever had.

* * * * *

When she awoke several hours later, Flare had left her once again. She leaned back against the pillows and savored the tug and pull of her sore muscles. She could almost feel Flare, still filling her with his cock.

Lounging lazily for a while, she had to force herself to get out of bed. She delved into the clothing she had brought and found a soft pair of jeans and a well-worn T-shirt, as well as some skimpy underthings that she knew Flare would approve of.

She couldn't wait for him to take them off her. Isis shivered with the delicious thought.

Seeking something useful to do while she waited for Flare to return, she tidied up the bedclothes and went to pick up all their discarded clothing from the past few days. Most of the clothing she had to throw away, putting it in a stone trashcan. As she gathered the last of the clothes, she couldn't help but notice the bits of paper that littered the floor. The last remnants of her past.

She gathered them up and threw them away—then alarm rushed through her. "Motherfucker," she said, searching through the bits of paper for her sister's envelope, which bore her return address. The address was missing. Isis looked under the bed and all around the room but she couldn't find it.

Holy shit," she cried out and ran for the door.

Chapter Fourteen

∽

Isis stepped into the hall and tried her best to ignore her ostentatious surroundings. She didn't want to be deterred from her important quest.

She'd never been outside Flare's apartment and she had a hopeless moment when she wondered just how she could find someone to help among all the doors lining the great stone hallway.

The hallway was wide enough to fit five school buses side by side. She looked down the hall and saw hundreds of doors, leading on as far as the eye could see. The stone around her was gray and dark, illuminated only by strange lights that haphazardly littered the passage. There were tapestries on the walls here and there, elaborate pieces of art full of color and life. There was statuary everywhere—carved into the rock of the walls. Everything looked inordinately expensive.

Barefoot and uncaring, she noticed the stone felt warm beneath her naked toes. Not at all cold. In fact, the air around her was a very pleasant, mild temperature. There was no noise in the hallway, just a pressing silence that unnerved her. There wasn't a Shikar to be seen anywhere. Realizing that if she was going to do anything she had to do it quick, she simply started knocking on doors.

After a dozen tries, someone answered her knock. It was a woman with long, curly red hair. "I need to find a Traveler. Now," Isis said urgently.

The woman eyed her curiously. "You're the new human among us," she said by way of greeting. "You are shorter than I expected." The woman said the words kindly so as not to offend.

"Look, I'm sorry I can't be more polite, but I *need* a Traveler."

"Why?" came a deep voice from behind her. Isis whirled and found herself face to chest with Pulse. He'd been standing so close behind her she wondered how she hadn't noticed his approach.

"Oh thank God," she said with a whoosh of breath. "I have to stop Flare from doing something really stupid," she told him quickly.

"Where is he?" Pulse asked, eyes puzzled.

"He's gone to my family's house. He intends to kill my stepfather."

Pulse's face showed that he had expected as much. "Perhaps the man deserves to die." He eyed her knowingly.

Isis ignored the look on his face — it would only have made her angry — and clutched the cloth of his shirt, ignoring the gasp from the woman behind her. "I have to stop him. Now," she gritted out, jerking the material hard.

"How do you intend to do that?" Pulse asked with infuriating indifference.

"Quit trying to stall me and find me a fucking Traveler," she growled. "If you don't, I'm going to tear this place apart looking for one."

The woman touched her shoulder. "This is The Generator. You shouldn't speak to him like that."

Pulse turned to the woman. "You may go now, Kittren," he said. The woman didn't say a word, simply turned and closed the door behind her firmly, shutting them outside in the great hallway, alone. Pulse turned back to her and Isis could have punched him for the look of male arrogance he gave her. "You shouldn't excite yourself so." He looked her over from head to toe. "You're a Shikar. So the transformation worked."

"Yes," she gritted out. "And you're going to know just how much a Shikar I can be if you don't tell me where to find a Traveler."

Pulse smiled slowly. "I can Travel," he told her. "And my spies have told me where your near-father can be found."

Isis felt her eyes go wide with surprise.

He chuckled. "I keep close tabs on all my warriors," he said patiently. "But I do not think you should interfere with Flare. Your near-father is an abomination. I say he deserves to die."

Panic made her shake and her eyes filled with tears. "Please. I have to stop him." She choked on the words. "I can't let him do this."

"I fear that Flare cannot be deterred. He went through a lot of trouble to find your family's home. Our spies had to locate the physical address he gave them before he could even Travel his way there. He is very determined."

"I know," she wailed. "But I have to try. Before it's too late."

Pulse eyed her silently for a long moment and she wondered what he was thinking. Seeming to come to a decision, he took her hand gently in his. "We'll go now," he assured her. "If you're certain you are ready."

"Yes. Take me there now," she told him in a rush.

The world disappeared in a way that she was growing quite familiar with now. The wild, flying feeling still made the bottom of her stomach drop out, and she still grew dizzy from the speed. But all the while she held tight to Pulse's hand and he seemed to impart some of his strength to her, keeping her alert.

They arrived in the big front yard of her parents' house. Isis felt the rough crabgrass beneath her naked feet. The place had gone to hell since her mother had died. Even though it was dark, she could easily see with her Shikar eyes the devastation that surrounded her.

The large flowerbeds her mother had been so proud of were gone. The grass was weedy and bare in many spots — something her mother would never have allowed. Junk cars lay dead along the sides of the long, gravel driveway. Trash and debris littered the ground everywhere.

The house was in no better condition. It looked like it might sink in on itself. The tin roof was rusted and ugly. The paint was peeling, revealing naked wood in many places. The porch sagged, the wood rotted through, and the smell of too many animals threatened to choke her. Isis had to make herself move, but she finally mustered the strength to approach the home she hadn't seen for almost ten years.

Pulse stayed close at her back. Isis was grateful for that, she realized. It gave her far more courage than she might have had under different circumstances.

On the porch, the screen door was hanging crookedly on its hinges, the old screen torn and ragged in many places. She opened it with trembling hands that betrayed her mounting trepidation. Dread weighted her heart as she realized she was about to see her hated family at long last.

The door was locked, but Isis didn't let that stop her. She slammed her palm against it and the door flew inward, its hinges creaking, broken with the force of her blow.

"Flare," she called out. There was no one in the sitting room—it had seemed such a big room when she was a child but now it looked pitifully small. She ignored the memories that assailed her. "Flare," she yelled more loudly.

"Who's there?" A voice came from down the hall that led to the bedrooms.

Isis took a reflexive step back then steeled her nerves as her stepfather walked into the room.

"Isis?" Jeff asked, surprise and fear entering his dark brown gaze. He flipped a switch and light flooded the room.

Isis looked at the man who had brought her so much suffering, but through different eyes than she'd possessed in her youth. He was shorter than she expected. Isis recalled that he'd had long hair when she'd left home, but now he was balding so that tufts of his grey hair stood up on end in patches all over his head.

Jeff was fatter than she remembered too. His gut hung out over his belt like a balloon filled with water.

His face was remarkably different from what she remembered and she realized it was because she had shattered his cheekbone that long-ago night. He'd had surgery to repair the damage—that much was apparent by the faint scars on his skin.

"What the hell are you doing here?" he snapped, coming toward her.

Isis realized with surprise that she stood taller than him now. She looked down at him as he approached her cautiously.

"You were never supposed to come back here," her stepfather said, anger and fear evident in his tone.

Then her stepfather noticed the tall, domineering presence of Pulse standing behind her silently in the darkness just outside the dwelling. Jeff gasped and took several panicked steps backward. The backs of his knees bumped into the old recliner that had been there since she was a kid, and he fell back against it clumsily.

"Is there a man here with you?" she asked as she gazed past Jeff, puzzled that Flare hadn't yet appeared.

"What the hell are you talking about? Fuck, you were always such a stupid kid," her stepfather snapped. "No one could ever understand a word you said."

Isis ignored his jab and turned to Pulse. "I don't understand. He's not here."

Pulse nodded his dark head. "I don't sense him anywhere near. Perhaps he hasn't arrived yet. He *was* on patrol for six hours, after all, and he may still be seeing to his duties."

"So what do I do? Just wait here for him?" she asked, at a loss.

"We can wait for him if you like. I have a feeling he won't be long," Pulse remarked, eyeing her stepfather with disgust. "Let's stand outside though. I cannot stomach this place or the company within it." He turned and led her out onto the porch once more. The cool night air hit her flushed cheeks and she welcomed the feel of it caressing her skin.

A splinter entered her foot from the rotted wood and Isis used the pain to help her focus on the task at hand. She did her best not to glance back at Jeff, but she couldn't resist the old familiar feeling in the pit of her stomach that she had always had in his presence. Her stomach felt as if she'd swallowed a lead cannonball. And her heart was beginning to ache painfully.

"Who's there, Dad?" Maria's voice surprised Isis into turning around to face her sister. She was heavy with child and fat besides. Her long titian hair, a mat of greasy strands on her head, drew Isis' gaze like a magnet. Maria looked as bad as Jeff. The beauty she had possessed as a child was no more than a shadow on her haggard, blemished face.

Maria took one look at Isis and a flame of pure hatred and malice lit up her light brown eyes. "What the fuck are you doing here, bitch?"

Isis gritted her teeth at her sister's high, shrieking voice. "I'm here to save Jeff's sorry life," she said with a patience she didn't feel.

Maria flew at her, and before Isis could react, her sister had raked her claws down her face. Isis fell back, not wanting to hurt her sister with her new strength. Isis was afraid that if she fought back she might kill Maria with a single blow.

Pulse came forward and caught Maria's hands before they could do any more damage. "Woman, you will not touch her again," he told her, shoving her roughly back.

Isis gently wiped the bloody claw marks on her face, wincing at the pain.

"You can't have him," her sister screamed in rage.

"I don't want him," Isis told her. "I *never* wanted him, can't you understand that?"

"Yes you did! Do you think I didn't see the looks you shared? Do you think I don't know about all the times you shared a bed with him? I saw it all, but I still won!" Her sister gave a horrible, shrieking laugh. "I've got him now and you can't take him from me!"

Maria launched herself once more at Isis, but this time Isis held out her hands and caught her sister's flailing ones within her fists. "Stop it, Maria." Isis spoke as forcefully as she could manage. "You're only making a fool of yourself."

"*I'm* a fool?" her sister shrieked. "You're the fool, you stupid, ugly bitch." She struggled and failed to reclaim her hands. Isis held her with an easy strength that surprised even her, keeping her at bay with little effort. Pulse had moved to stand behind her once more, lending her his strength should Isis have need of it. But Isis was strong enough on her own. Flare had taught her that.

"Sit down, Maria," she said stonily, pushing her away so that her sister stumbled and sat down, hard, on the couch. "I don't want to hurt you," Isis said patiently.

"I don't care if you fight back or not, I'm still going to kick your ass," Maria choked out in a shrill voice that grated harshly on Isis' Shikar-sensitive ears.

Isis tried to appeal to her sister's reasoning. "You're pregnant. You shouldn't try to fight me. You could hurt the baby."

"Fuck you, bitch!" Her sister physically spat at Isis but missed her mark. "You're just jealous that this is my baby and not yours."

Isis gave up. She turned her back on her sister and went out onto the porch again, looking out into the distance. "Maybe he won't come. Maybe he changed his mind."

Pulse looked over her head and smiled. "I would say that is a fanciful notion, my dear," he said.

Isis turned and saw Flare standing behind her, inside the house. Both her stepfather and her sister were staring at him with dumbfounded looks on their faces as he appeared before their eyes like magic.

"Flare," she said, approaching his side. Her relief at seeing him safe lasted only long enough for her fear of what he intended to do to take hold. "Don't do this," she begged.

Flare was so hot Isis could actually see the waves of heat washing from him. "He deserves to die for what he did to you," Flare said from behind clenched teeth. He put out his hand and gently wiped away the blood still oozing from the claw marks on her face. Isis felt a gentle heat and her skin healed instantly. Flare turned from her and looked down at Jeff with a sneer. "So you're the bastard who hurts defenseless children."

"No," Isis cried, but it was too late. Flare grabbed her stepfather's neck and lifted him clear off his feet with an easy strength. With a flick of his wrist Flare threw him out the living room window. Wood and glass flew and the house groaned like it might collapse at any moment.

Isis ran out the door, beating Flare to her stepfather's fallen form, struggling to get up from the hard ground. "Stop it, Flare," she said, putting herself between the only two men who had ever mattered in her life. "I mean it." Flare ignored her and gently pushed her away. He looked down at Jeff once again. Flare reached for the cowering man and punched him—right where Isis had punched him years before. Isis heard the bones fracturing in his cheek and she winced reflexively.

She pulled at Flare. "This is stupid and pointless," she said in an effort to coax him away from his death grip on her stepfather's head. Flare slammed Jeff's head to the ground and Isis feared for a moment that Flare had killed him. Her stepfather went limp and lifeless beneath Flare, alarming her further.

Flare stood back with disgust. "He's passed out. The cowardly bastard."

Isis took the opportunity to take one of his hands in hers. "Let's go home. You've punished him enough. We can go now. We don't ever have to think about these people again."

Maria screamed and ran out of the house, charging Isis. Flare reached out and grabbed the woman by the material of her shirt at the nape of her neck. "You are with child and I will not strike you. But I warn you, keep your hands off my mate," he commanded the shrieking woman.

Maria immediately quieted and Flare released her, her fear of him more than apparent. Jeff moaned behind them, attracting Flare's attention once again. Isis grabbed onto Flare's shirt, but she didn't hold on for long.

Something didn't feel right. Beyond the fact that she was trying to keep Flare from killing her worthless excuse for a dad, she felt a slowly growing alarm wash through her.

The feeling of a thousand feathers tickling her brain made her lose focus. There was a dead weight in her chest that stole her breath and her heart raced.

"Flare," she said slowly, looking around her for the threat she knew lingered nearby.

"Flare," she called again when he didn't answer her.

"What is it?" Pulse had heard the new tone of worry in her voice.

"Daemons," she said, shaking. "We're about to have some company."

Chapter Fifteen

ॐ

The ground rumbled beneath her feet. "What was that?"

Pulse looked around and Flare immediately left his position by the slowly awakening Jeff. Neither of the two Shikars answered her question. They stood side by side, legs braced apart, both looking ready to do battle.

"Do you see anything?" Isis asked them both.

The ground rolled, sending all of them stumbling. A horrible, deep roaring sound filled her ears and slammed into her chest with an almost physical force. The feeling of her skin stretching taught over her bones intensified and she shivered uncontrollably. The roaring continued, deafening as it grew louder, closer, but Isis couldn't see where the threat was coming from.

She didn't have a chance to. The ground beneath her feet rose several feet, throwing her off balance so that she fell back. The ground sank then rose again as something broke through it with such violence that it audibly shook the house on its foundation.

A great, giant worm-looking thing surged into the sky, its body speeding from the hole in the ground endlessly, as if the thing were miles long. On the back of the worm's neck was a Daemon—larger than any she'd seen before—and it was riding the worm with ease, a leather stirrup held in his hand, the end of it pierced through the head of the worm to keep it in place and to allow the Daemon complete control of the creature.

"What the fuck is that?" Isis surged to her feet with an alien speed that astonished her.

"That is a Canker-Worm," Flare said. "Get back, Isis."

Isis felt her Foils pierce through the skin of her fingertips. Ignoring Flare's warning, she jumped on the back of the worm and dug her blades into the disgusting mess that was the worm's flesh. Flare jumped the same time as she, landing on a different part of the worm's massive body, and shoved his own red-hot Foils into the monstrosity.

The Canker-Worm let out a booming cry that vibrated Isis' skull.

Flames spread out from where Flare pierced the worm and ran a great length down the monster's body. Isis pulled her claws out and sank them deep again. And again. And again. Soon she was covered head to toe with the beast's blood and gore, yet still she fought on.

The worm slammed onto the grass, shaking the earth, its tail still stuck in the hole it had made for itself in the ground. The move threw Isis around and her legs flew out behind her. Only her Foils, buried deep, kept her from launching into the air.

The Daemon that rode the beast jumped her. She'd forgotten about this beast while she'd pounded on the worm. It grabbed her hair, pulling out strands so that she cried out with pain. Then all pain was forgotten as she grew angrier and angrier, almost reflexively. With a roar of rage, she lunged back at the Daemon and sank her arms elbow deep into its rib cage.

The Daemon shrieked a horrible sound and threw her off. This time her Foils did not save her and she fell to the ground with a thud. But she was not deterred in the least. She rose swiftly and jumped back onto the worm. It was flailing madly, but she managed to race up its unsteady length to where the Daemon waited and Isis engaged it in battle once more.

The Daemon landed a blow to the side of her head that made her see stars. Feeling her anger mount to unbelievable highs, a large Foil grew from her wrist. It looked like the blade of a glowing great sword in the darkness. With one swipe of the blade she took the Daemon's head. Then, wasting no time, she plunged her hand back into its chest and sought out its heart, tearing it free when she found it.

She tore the heart in half with one tug of her hands.

Tossing the organ over her shoulder, she watched as the Daemon fell, dead, to the ground. Isis ignored it, bent down and drove the sword in her wrist into the worm once again. The great beast shuddered and screamed its rage and pain into the night—the sound like a thousand nails scraping down a chalkboard all at once.

Isis had forgotten about Pulse. The man walked with a casual grace to stand at the mouth of the worm. "Clear," he shouted and both Isis and Flare flung themselves from the beast. Pulse raised his hands and a thick bolt of lightning streaked down from the sky.

It hit the worm's head dead center. The worm screamed and lunged at Pulse, who easily sidestepped its attack with alarming speed. Another bolt came down with a clashing sound, and all the hairs on Isis' body rose from the static electricity in the night air. This bolt too hit the worm's head, singeing its brain to nothing. The gigantic worm fell limp, dead, with one last mighty groan that shook the earth.

Flare held his hands out and liquid fire poured forth—his hands were like two great flamethrowers—and the flames engulfed the once mighty beast. The smell of stinking, rotting, burning flesh filled the air, choking Isis, making her gag. Flare found the fallen form of the Daemon and immediately set it aflame too.

The three Shikars stood and watched as the carcasses of their enemies burned. They were reduced to ash within ten minutes, the bodies destroyed by the intense heat of Flare's fire. The smell of it, however, lingered like a bad memory.

Isis at once became aware of the chirping sound of crickets in the night. Her anger cooled and she tried to pull the sword Foil back within her body. She didn't know how to do it. She tried over and over again, willing it to retract, frustrating herself.

"I can't make this go away," she growled, shaking her hand as if that would dislodge the blade.

Flare looked over at her, relief filling his eyes now that he knew Isis was going to be all right after her ordeal. He smiled at her warmly. "It'll retract. Don't fight it so," he instructed her.

Isis let her hand fall to her side and the blade of her Foil scraped the dirt on the ground, jarring her. Isis looked around her at the devastation. There was a mammoth hole in the ground and ash and soot were everywhere, covering everything in a thick coat of the horrible stuff.

Looking around for her family, Isis found them huddled together on the ground beside the porch. "Are you all right?" she asked, caring only that Maria's baby hadn't been placed in any danger.

Neither of them answered. Instead they huddled there, clutching each other desperately, panting and moaning as if what they had just seen had driven them mad.

"Get away from them, Isis," Flare commanded. He put his arm on her shoulder and pulled her back against him. Flare eyed her family disdainfully. "They look great there together, cowering like children. Don't you think?"

Isis chuckled and turned, placing her hand on Flare's chest and tracing little circles on his pecs. "Let's leave them here to clean up this mess," she said. "I think they've been through enough tonight."

Flare looked as if he wanted to argue. Isis shushed him with a finger at his lips. "Just let it go. I have," she said. "You never have to think about them again. I know I won't."

Her Shikar warrior kissed her gently on the temple. "If that is your wish."

"It is," she said with a relieved breath, grateful that he would not push the matter.

Pulse came to stand beside them. "I have no such duty to see to your pleasure, Isis. So here is my gift to them." Lightning streaked out of the sky, hitting the dilapidated house, setting it instantly ablaze. "There. I feel better all ready." Pulse chuckled as he watched his own handiwork play out. Then he sobered and as the sky brightened with the light of the blaze that was now roaring through the old house, he turned to his comrades.

"Let's go home," he said. "I must tell the Council about this incident. Canker-Worms are not at all common on the surface. They are most difficult to capture and there's not enough methane in the air to sustain them up here for long. The Daemons went through a lot of trouble to claim you, Isis. I think in time we'll know why. Once your powers blossom."

Isis entwined her fingers with Flame's and looked up at him from behind a tangle of her hair, which did nothing to shield her from the sight of her childhood home burning down around them. "Let's go home now," she urged.

Flare gathered her close, gave one last disgusted look at her still-cowering family, and took her forever away from the place of her greatest suffering.

* * * * *

They arrived, alone, back in Flare's apartment. Pulse had chosen a different route to Travel, no doubt to afford them the privacy they needed, and was nowhere to be seen.

"You should have let me kill him," Flare murmured into her hair as she settled into his strong embrace.

"I think it's better this way. What they saw tonight will trouble both my stepdad and my sister for a long time to come. I say let them suffer through it, with no answers to explain away their fears."

Flare grinned down at her. "That scenario is quite amusing to think on, is it not?"

Isis locked her gaze with his. "I am never going to think about them again," she said firmly.

She could tell by the look in his eyes that he was proud of her resolve, even if he did still want to kill her stepfather. With a wince, her Foil retracted back into her bones and she flexed her hand wonderingly that it had not pained her at all.

"Come on," she said, tugging him along. "Let's take a bath and get all this crap off us."

Flare's wicked smile did something magical to her insides. "Let's."

They helped each other undress and put their clothes in a bin whose contents, Flare told her, was collected and washed by some of the women. They filled the tub with hot, steaming water and they both groaned their delight as they sank into the liquid. Their muscles relaxed, their cares and worries of the day washed away. Isis scrubbed herself vigorously and Flare was no different. Soon the bathwater was black with impurities.

They climbed out of the bath and Flare dried her off with another of his ultra-plush towels before drying himself off in that strange way of his. Once the flames had died down he held her tight against him, kissed her softly on the lips and lifted her easily in his arms.

Isis rained kisses along the strong ridge of his jaw. Her hands roved hungrily over his hot naked skin, reveling in its hard, unyielding smoothness beneath her fingertips.

Flare laid her down on the bed and spread her legs with his strong, rough hands. He immediately bent his head and darted his tongue out to taste her. He lingered, using his lips, teeth and tongue to torment her. Isis cried out and clutched his head to her, writhing beneath his wicked kiss.

He stayed with her, lips nibbling at her clit, his tongue delving deep. He replaced his tongue with two fingers, stretching and penetrating her, feeling the quaking of her form around his hand. He licked her clit then sucked upon it, making her scream and thrash and pull his head even closer with desperate hands.

Minutes later he showed no sign that he would stop his sweet torture. Isis felt like her skin was swollen all over, full of sensations that stole her thoughts and her breath away. Her hips bucked against him as his teeth scraped her clit. When his fingers unerringly found her G-spot, scraping back and forth across it with the rough pads of his fingers, she came up off the bed with a roar and instantly climaxed.

Chuckling his satisfaction, he pushed her back down onto the bed and claimed her lips. The taste of her was heady on his tongue and she moaned around his probing. He was so hot that Isis was sweating from the stifling heat in the room. Flare darted his tongue out to capture a bead of her sweat from her brow before returning to her lips to tease and torment her mercilessly.

His fingers toyed with her breasts. Squeezing the plump globes before tweaking her overly sensitive nipples, he settled himself between her open legs. He found her core and surged into her, making them both gasp and quake with lust.

Isis threw her arms around his neck and kissed him with all the passion she possessed. Their breath mingled, their hair tangled together and their bodies slid against each other, eased by the slipperiness of her sweat-coated body.

"You mean everything to me," he murmured against her passion-swollen lips.

Isis clutched him tighter to her and wrapped her legs around his waist. She met him thrust for thrust, gasping and moaning breathlessly. Her fingernails dug into the skin of his back, leaving little half moons behind in his flesh. Flare growled and thrust harder, faster into her.

They came at the same time, their bodies truly one in that moment of utmost bliss. Isis screamed and her body milked him of his seed. Flare growled and let her have all of him, holding her close.

"You're mine," he said firmly, possessively.

Isis could only nod as she fell limp against the mattress underneath her. "I'll always be yours," she whispered moments later.

Flare gathered her close and they settled into bed. In the space of a few breaths they were both asleep in each other's arms, Flare's warmth soothing her into the deep relaxation of one loved and cherished by her mate.

Epilogue

Months passed and Isis spent most of her waking hours honing her Shikar skills. It had become apparent that she would be a Hunter Caste from the first, but she still needed to learn to control her Foils and her incredible strength. It wasn't easy, yet the time passed as swiftly as if it had wings.

Isis and Flare spent all their nights together talking, making love and learning more about each other with each passing day. She and Flare moved out of his apartment and moved into a new one deeper within the city—specifically designed to meet Flare's requirements, plus a few of her own. They made their home together and there was much talk of the future.

Flare wanted children. Isis wasn't ready. So they struck a bargain. Once Isis turned thirty they would consider starting a family together. In the meanwhile they enjoyed each other's company immensely. They seemed a perfect match—their temperaments not as dissimilar as they might have thought in the beginning.

Isis met several more Shikars. And each one was as beautiful as a flower in bloom—their genes much more complicated than a human's. A woman by the name of Agate helped to train her in the afternoons—teaching her to hone her Hunting instincts. During the day she practiced rigorously with her Foils, finally grasping the art of unsheathing and retracting blades through her skin.

She no longer thought about her past. It was wiped clean from her thoughts as if it had never been. Her heart healed and she grew more confident in herself, learning to make a home out of her and Flare's new apartment. Making the first real home she'd ever known. It was far more wonderful than she ever could have imagined, simply being a part of the Shikar world.

There were no more nightmares. Flare had banished those with his endless love for her. Isis no longer felt alone, cut adrift. She felt like she was part of something grand and magical, and she was. Everything about the Shikar way of life interested her and soon she'd overcome her antisocial behavior and made friends with their neighbors, especially with her instructor, Agate. Isis had never had a friend and it was a heartwarming experience, one she treasured.

Flare went back to his patrolling of the Territories. He was gone for six hours every day, but Isis grew used to the separation. While Flare was gone she decorated their home and trained, honing her body into a fighting machine, a weapon.

One day, Flare invited her to join him on the surface world. Isis jumped at the chance. Before she could go, however, she was required to wear the strange, latex-like paint that served as a strong armor against bodily damage. She wore it under her clothes, growing used to it like she might a second skin. When she was ready, Flare took her hand and Traveled to the land of the Territories.

They arrived in Hawaii at dusk. Isis could tell where they were by the flora of the land and the crystal clear ocean along the coast. Flare took her hand and led her deep into a vegetated area. Minutes later they came to a clearing and Isis gasped in surprise at what was waiting for them there.

The area was littered with blossoms of every hue and texture. A big, soft bed of white rose petals lay under the shade of a palm tree, awaiting them. She looked at Flare with pleasant surprise.

"I don't have to patrol tonight. I thought maybe you would like coming here with me."

"You did all this?"

Flare smiled at her tenderly and traced a fingertip down her soft cheek. "For you," he answered.

Isis laughed delightedly before regaining her control. She eyed Flare seductively and turned away from him. Without urging from her mate she began to dance for him. She sensually removed all of her clothing, stripping down to nothing, teasing him mercilessly with her decadent performance. Flare shucked his clothing in record time and before she could blink he had tackled her to the ground, turning at the last minute so he took the impact of their landing onto himself.

The smell of roses filled their senses, making them drunk with desire. Isis straddled Flare and ran her hands all over his chest and belly, reveling in the feel of him between her legs. His cocked rubbed deliciously in the wet channel of her pussy, but Isis was careful not to let him penetrate her. At least, not *yet*.

Flare grabbed a fistful of rose petals and flung them into the air. They showered down upon their hot, eager bodies like a soft rain. Some of the petals tangled in their hair, making them both look like exotic wood nymphs.

"I love you," she said and kissed his left nipple, teasing it with her tongue.

"And I love you," he returned with a moan, his own fingers seeking her breasts to toy and play with her thick, erect nipples. "More than you'll ever know," he finished breathlessly.

They both lost the ability to speak as passion took control. Flare ran his hands all over her body, pausing to squeeze her breasts and her ass roughly. He pulled her hair, making her lower her head for his kiss. His tongue entered her like the caress of a flame and she suckled gently upon it, fusing their mouths together.

Flare's fingers moved between their bodies and found her clit. It was swollen and aching and he dipped his finger lower to gather Isis' own moisture to ease his caress over the tiny nubbin of flesh. Electricity shot through her and she cried out, moving on his hand uncontrollably, undulating her hips in a way she knew would drive him wild.

His body thrust into hers, filling her completely. Isis shrieked her pleasure and arched into his movement, welcoming the thick weight of his cock within her body. There was no more tenderness between them—both were too eager for that. Isis rode him hard, rotating her hips on him, bouncing up and down on his wet, glistening cock.

Those magic finger of his teased her, one at her nipple, one on her clit. Before she knew it she was moaning over and over and with one, violent thrust she came around him.

Flare arched up into her and found his own release, shouting his triumph to the heavens as he spurted deep within her. He sat up and took one of her breasts deep into his mouth. He was still hard inside her and before too many seconds had passed he was moving inside of her once again.

He rolled them, pressing her down into the soft bed of rose petals. He spread out her hair to admire its bright fire among the white petals. Taking hold of her ankles, he put her feet on his shoulders, tilting her just so, so that he could penetrate her more deeply.

The feel of his cock rubbing against her G-spot made her wild so that she rode him faster and faster, reveling in the exquisite sensation. Flare's body temperature soared, especially in his cock. It burned her delicately, buried deep inside of her, and she came again. Hard.

She screamed, pulling at his hair and arms, clutching for anything that would keep her from going insane with her overwhelming pleasure. Flare grunted and shoved harder into her, stretching and filling her body even as it milked him with her tremors of release.

The petals around them singed to black and fragrant smoke rose to tickle their noses. Flare came down inside of her one last time and shot his load within her again with a long, ragged moan. Isis felt the heat of his seed wash into her and she relished every second of his ecstasy.

When they had both come to their senses, the entire bower of flowers had been singed to ash. Isis looked at him, eyebrow raised, toying with him. "At least *I* didn't catch fire," she remarked with a chuckle.

"What can I say, you make me lose control," he said sheepishly. He withdrew his body from hers and gathered her close. He kissed her lips, tasting her deep recesses with his tongue. They lay that way for hours, until the dawn had crept up over the horizon.

"Let's go home," he told her at last.

Home. Something Isis had never in her wildest dreams imagined she could have. "Let's," she said, taking his hand.

The world fell away, but they were together, hands and fingers entwined. And that was all that mattered.

Enjoy an excerpt from:
RIDE THE LIGHTNING

Copyright © SHERRI L. KING, 2006.
All Rights Reserved, Ellora's Cave Publishing, Inc.

§

Luna Boone was waiting for a tragedy to happen.

In her twenty-four years of life she had seen much—
and not all of it was pretty. She was used to seeing the
very worst side of human nature, the bestial creatures all
humans were deep down inside. More than most, she
knew that beneath the sliver of our higher brains lies a
reptilian brain that wants nothing more than to fight and
maim. Luna accepted this, yet still she was hopeful that
she could change things.

Her hopefulness was naturally sometimes shaken by
despair. But she refused to become weak and
despondent, as her mother had been. The road to
weakness led only to madness, and she just wasn't ready
to give up control of her resolve quite yet.

The world was a dark and dangerous place with
many hidden secrets and twisted desires. Luna had been
taught that since the cradle and she truly believed it
some of the time. But she *wanted* to believe otherwise.
Desperately. She wanted to see the beauty and innocence
in the world. She knew it must be there somewhere—
and she *would* find it, if only she searched hard enough.

Will I be strong enough to see this through? she
wondered. Would this be the time that she finally
changed things? Her brain itched with questions and
none of them had answers, at least none that Luna could
see. She would simply have to wait and watch and find
out. She glanced at her watch for what must have been
the hundredth time since arriving on the street corner in
front of the Times Square Hilton.

Fifteen minutes left.

Luna didn't know how she was going to prevent it
from happening. She'd never before succeeded in
changing the outcome of her predictions, only little

pieces of them that seemed to have no real effect on the end result. Still, she had to try. She was the only one who knew it would happen and thus it was her responsibility to try and change things. It was her gift and her curse and she must do her part, whatever that was.

For many years she'd done her best to prevent the premonitions from coming true, but it had been a fruitless endeavor. Fate, it seemed, was already written and Luna had no idea how to rewrite it. Yet there was still a desperate need in her to *try*. This, too, was part of her curse.

It wouldn't be easy, fighting to prevent the tragedy. But she would persevere and hold fast to her courage despite the odds, despite the near certainty that she would fail. She always did, even if it didn't do anyone else any good.

Out of the corner of her eye she saw a black shape exit the hotel. Why this shadow caught her attention, turning it away from her true mission, she couldn't have said. But the man in black was something she'd never encountered before. She almost couldn't believe her eyes.

He was handsome as all get out—that, of course, caught her attention first. The black hair on his head was long, down to the middle of his back and unbound. The wind teased the strands and tiny streaks of silver glinted in the lights. The exotic vision of it held her mesmerized for precious seconds when she should have been thinking on what was about to happen.

Yet still Luna couldn't help watching him. He was dressed strangely, in a soft, loose-fitting tunic and equally soft-looking pants, but the style was foreign, like none she was familiar with. He had boots on his feet, shiny and black with tarnished silver buckles that did nothing to disguise how big his feet were. In fact, all of him was big, she realized. He had to stand just a few inches below seven feet. Luna had never seen someone as tall as he in person, only on televised basketball games. He presented quite an imposing figure of masculine strength.

His shoulders were shockingly broad and undoubtedly strong. He had a handsome face, a surprisingly square jaw and a long, strong nose. Smooth, unblemished skin the rich color of bronze indicated he was definitely not Caucasian, or at least if he was it was mixed with something else more exotic. His midnight-dark brows flared artfully over his brown eyes and—

His eyes weren't brown. She knew it—suddenly and with a familiar certainty.

Curious, she watched as a vagrant approached the man, begging for money. She felt her eyes bulge when the man quite unexpectedly handed the vagrant a thick wad of bills. The vagrant nearly fainted, blubbering his thanks before swiftly departing, no doubt fearing the dark stranger would change his mind and take the money back.

Luna approached the odd stranger as if magnetically drawn to him, leaving her post by the bustling street—something she would never, ever have done before. She couldn't help herself—her instincts were practically singing an aria and she could do no less than indulge her curiosity.

"He's going to spend that on booze, you know. He'll be dead in two months from alcohol poisoning," she told him by way of greeting.

The man glanced down at her as if he'd never seen another human being before and she instinctively took a step back. There was an arrogance and disdain in his eyes that Luna didn't like one bit. He looked as if he owned the world, and the people in it were only living there because he allowed them to.

Feeling a thrill of that "other" awareness that was so much a part of her, she glanced at her watch, tearing her eyes away from his artificially colored ones with great effort. Ten minutes to go.

Despite the urgency driving her, Luna eyed him once more, her gaze drawn to him as if by a force greater than her will. She wondered just what it was about him that had caught her attention. It was true that he was probably the best-looking man she'd ever seen, but it was more than that, and Luna had long ago learned to trust her instincts. And right now her instincts demanded she pay attention to this stranger.

A figurative light dawned in her mind and she gasped softly in surprise before she could swallow the revealing sound. The man had looked away from her during the few seconds of her revelation, taking in his surroundings like a thirsty sponge. And it was no wonder. Luna doubted he'd been on Earth for very long.

Why an electronic book?

We live in the Information Age—an exciting time in the history of human civilization, in which technology rules supreme and continues to progress in leaps and bounds every minute of every day. For a multitude of reasons, more and more avid literary fans are opting to purchase e-books instead of paper books. The question from those not yet initiated into the world of electronic reading is simply: *Why?*

1. *Price.*   An electronic title at Ellora's Cave Publishing and Cerridwen Press runs anywhere from 40% to 75% less than the cover price of the exact same title in paperback format. Why? Basic mathematics and cost. It is less expensive to publish an e-book (no paper and printing, no warehousing and shipping) than it is to publish a paperback, so the savings are passed along to the consumer.

2. *Space.*   Running out of room in your house for your books? That is one worry you will never have with electronic books. For a low one-time cost, you can purchase a handheld device specifically designed for e-reading. Many e-readers have large, convenient screens for viewing. Better yet, hundreds of titles can be stored within your new library—on a single microchip. There are a variety of e-readers from different manufacturers. You can also read e-books on your PC or laptop computer. (Please note that Ellora's Cave does not endorse any specific brands. You can check our websites at www.ellorascave.com

or www.cerridwenpress.com for information we make available to new consumers.)

3. *Mobility.* Because your new e-library consists of only a microchip within a small, easily transportable e-reader, your entire cache of books can be taken with you wherever you go.

4. *Personal Viewing Preferences.* Are the words you are currently reading too small? Too large? Too... ANNOYING? Paperback books cannot be modified according to personal preferences, but e-books can.

5. *Instant Gratification.* Is it the middle of the night and all the bookstores near you are closed? Are you tired of waiting days, sometimes weeks, for bookstores to ship the novels you bought? Ellora's Cave Publishing sells instantaneous downloads twenty-four hours a day, seven days a week, every day of the year. Our webstore is never closed. Our e-book delivery system is 100% automated, meaning your order is filled as soon as you pay for it.

Those are a few of the top reasons why electronic books are replacing paperbacks for many avid readers.

As always, Ellora's Cave and Cerridwen Press welcome your questions and comments. We invite you to email us at Comments@ellorascave.com or write to us directly at Ellora's Cave Publishing Inc., 1056 Home Avenue, Akron, OH 44310-3502.

Make each day more EXCITING with our
Ellora's Cavemen
Calendar
www.EllorasCave.com